JONAH

Also by Ellen Gunderson Traylor in Large Print:

Melchizedek

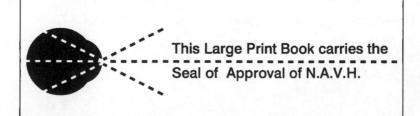

This Large Print Book carries the Seal of Approval of N.A.V.H.

JONAH

ELLEN GUNDERSON TRAYLOR

Thorndike Press • Waterville, Maine

Published in 2002 by arrangement with Tyndale House
Publishers, Inc.

Thorndike Press Large Print Christian Fiction Series.

The tree indicium is a trademark of Thorndike Press.

The text of this Large Print edition is unabridged.
Other aspects of the book may vary from the original edition.

Cover design by Thorndike Press Staff.

Set in 16 pt. Plantin by Warren S. Doersam.

Printed in the United States on permanent paper.

Library of Congress Control Number: 2002092263
ISBN 0-7862-4577-8 (lg. print : hc : alk. paper)

To my littlest boy

NATHAN

who loves big fishes

CONTENTS

But [Jesus] answered and said unto them,
An evil and adulterous generation
seeketh after a sign; and there
shall no sign be given to it,
but the sign of the prophet Jona[h].

MATTHEW 12:39

ASSYRIAN EMPIRE
(782 B.C. & following)

Capital

Nineveh (Dog of the Tigris,
Bloody Dog,
Warlords of the East,
Eastern Dog)

Emperors

Adad-Nirari III
Shalmaneser IV
Ashur-dan (sister, Kisha)

Vassal Nations

Syria (capital, Damascus;
king, Ben-Hadad)

Israel (capital, Samaria;
kings, Joash, Jeroboam
[queen, Marna]; priest, Amaziah)

Judah (capital, Jerusalem;
king, Uzziah)

Israel and Judah together
were called *Palestine*,
and their people were called *Hebrews*.

HEBREW PROPHETS

Elisha

Amos of Tekoa,
Judah (mission to Israel)

Jonah of Gath-hepher,
Israel (mission to
Israel and Nineveh)

GODS

Jehovah (Hebrews)

Asshur (Ninevites)

PROLOGUE

There is a little mound in the desert alongside the Tigris River, where once the great
city of Nineveh stood. It is situated beside
the site of the city's old western wall, which
has now crumbled into unrecognizable
decay. And though the ancient and glorious
metropolis, which sparked a thousand legends and was Assyria's crowning gem, shall
never rise again, the smaller hump of earth
which rests within its vanquished borders
still stirs the imagination of those who pass
by.

For it is the tomb of a prophet.

Nebi Yunas the mound is called: "Tomb
of the Prophet Jonah."

How, one wonders, did a Hebrew seer
come to dwell in this heathen place, not
only to preach here and declare the judgment of God on the city's wickedness, but
to live out his days within its pagan walls?

The story of Jonah, who was "swallowed
by a great fish," is one of the most popular
tales in the Bible.

But the saga of this man, the first "missionary," is one of far grander scale than just the episode at sea. His is a tale of two nations, and of two kings, of a period unsurpassed for glory, war, and oppression. This is a tale, also, of two prophets, and of the mantle that was passed between them.

Were we to sit at Jonah's feet, beside the Nineveh gate, and to hear his account of the story, it would be interwoven with a wealth of royal names and far-flung places, reflecting the height of glamour and the pit of despondency. For his tale bridges two continents, the rise and fall of conquerors, and the work of God at the heart of two empires.

Jonah's feet, which for a time ran in rebellion from Jehovah, eventually learned obedience and carried him to proclaim a wondrous message to those who sat in darkness.

But God's greatest work took place in Jonah's spirit. For he, whose heart had once been narrow, grew to encompass the unlovely.

We would, if we were privileged to talk with him, see his eyes light up with love as he spoke of Amos, his fellow prophet; of Ashur-dan, the feared emperor of Assyria;

and of Jeroboam, king of Israel.

"Jeroboam, son of Joash," he would whisper. "This is his story, as well as mine. . . ."

PART ONE

THE CALL
AND
THE CLOAK

*Surely the Lord God
will do nothing, but
he revealeth his secret
unto his servants
the prophets.
The lion hath roared,
who will not fear? the
Lord God hath
spoken, who can but
prophesy?*

AMOS 3:7, 8

CHAPTER
1

782 B.C.

Clouds of spikenard incense wafted across the king's balcony, drifting into the Samaritan night like breaths of a chant. Inside the dark chamber, censers swung from golden chains in cadence to the priests' prayers, and in obedience to their swaying hands, catching faint light from yellow lampstands about the room.

The song of the holy men was a dirge — though Joash, king of Israel, was not yet dead. His son, pacing the little porch, tried to ignore the supplications, which pleaded for Jehovah's kindness on the old man's soul. The strapping youngster cared not to think on Jehovah, and rebelled against the intercessors. If his father's time to die had come, he reasoned, it was too late to plead for anything.

"A hard God you are," he muttered, "implacable and hard. . . ." Tears stung his brooding eyes as he looked south toward Jerusalem, capital of his father's rival, Judah — Israel's sister kingdom and bloody foe.

Had the Lord not recently blessed Joash with great victory? Had he not given him power to break down the walls of David's city to four hundred cubits? Israel had taken booty from the Temple of Solomon and from Jerusalem's palace, as well as many hostages. Yet now the king lay dying, unable to savor the glory that had been so dearly won.

The prince turned his gaze north, toward the mountains of Syria, where his father had thrice defeated Ben-Hadad. Three times he had proven his prowess, and the hand of the Lord was with him. But the right to utterly destroy the desert dwellers had been revoked.

"By the whim of Jehovah . . ." The prince spat. "By the whim of your prophet!"

The rasping sounds of his father's uneven breathing mingled with the chants and filled the prince's ears. He remembered the story of the death of Elisha, prophet of God, rehearsed countless times by the king — how Joash had sped to his side at his last moments, to the deathbed of his beloved friend.

"My father!" the king had cried upon finding him. And throwing himself beside the prophet, weeping sore, he had pleaded, "My father, my father, the chariots of Israel and its horsemen!"

Raising a wizened hand, and running gnarled fingers through Joash's hair, Elisha had groaned, "No, my son, there is no army now to save me. I go to Jehovah. And may my going be with speed."

Directing the king's attention to the soldiers who accompanied him, he had pointed to their weapons of war.

"Take a bow and arrows," the prophet commanded.

Joash had done so, wonderingly.

"Yes — put your hand upon the bow," Elisha ordered.

Joash obeyed, holding the bow between himself and his mentor. His eyes insistent, the old prophet reached forth, placing his callused hands upon the king's.

"Open the window toward the east," Elisha directed.

Trembling, Joash again obeyed.

"Shoot!"

And he did.

Rising up on one elbow, the old seer had watched the flint's arc, and his ancient eyes had widened. "The Lord's arrow," he had cried, "even the arrow of victory over Syria!"

Joash had turned to him, incredulous. Then, with fist lifted toward heaven, Elisha had declared, "For you shall smite the Syrians at Aphek until you have destroyed them!"

The prophet's gaze had then plumbed the depths of the king's soul, as if reading whether he were fit for the challenge. But Joash had been silent, his heart full of dread.

"Take the arrows," Elisha had ordered, pointing to a full quiver.

Joash had done so, fearing his intention. And then, reaching forth, Elisha had rested his old hand upon the king's head, pressing him firmly toward the floor.

"Strike the ground!" the prophet cried.

Joash, sensing that the success of the prophecy depended on his willingness, shivered beneath the hand. "A sign of covenant?" he asked weakly.

"It is," Elisha asserted. "Strike the ground."

The great cities of Syria, including its capital Damascus, flashed to the king's mind, one by one, his inner vision moving steadily north. It would start at Aphek, he knew, for the prophet had said so. He was not afraid of such a battle. Bravely he struck the ground.

The prophet nodded approval, then waited. Joash knew what was required. To advance further would necessitate going against Ashtaroth and Karnaim. This he could do, without risk. With a sturdy sigh, he struck the ground twice more.

He sought Elisha's favor, and found it on his face. But then he trembled, for he knew the prophet was not satisfied.

"Damascus?" he whispered. "Hamath?"

There was no reply. He knew the answer. If he were to utterly destroy Syria, it would require his trespass into the region over which Assyria, mightiest empire on earth, held formal sway. For Syria, though powerful, had bowed her territorial knee, relinquishing land from Damascus north through Hamath to the Taurus mountains, and east to the Euphrates. Though the monarch of Damascus, Ben-Hadad, was not a threat to Joash, he was a vassal of the eastern hawks, the imperial warlords beyond the Euphrates.

Who was Israel to invade imperial borders? Was she not herself a vassal of Assyria? Had not the king of Nineveh, capital of the world, said, "Thus far shall you go and no farther"?

No, Joash considered, *I cannot invade Damascus.*

Not daring to look the prophet in the eye, the Israelite stood up from the floor.

Of course the holy man was angered at such cowardice. Ripping the arrows from Joash's grasp, he had snarled, "You should have struck five or six times! Then you would have smitten Syria until you made an end of her. But now," his eyes clouded, "you shall strike Syria only three times, and not within her weakest joints."

"Weakest?" Joash had countered, his own anger piqued despite his regard for Elisha. "How can you call Damascus and Hamath weak? Are they not protected by Nineveh?"

At this Elisha had lain back upon his bed, shaking his hoary head. "You have not acted in faith," he corrected. "All the empires of the world cannot stand against one man of God."

With this, Elisha had breathed his last, and Joash had crumpled to his knees beside him. Tears of remorse and grief could not change matters. But he shed them, nonetheless.

Remembering this tale, the prince, son of Joash, still paced the balcony, fists clenched as he attempted to make sense of Jehovah's ways. Blessed as his father was, he had not been allowed to realize his greatest potential. Syria still reigned to the north; and stretching from the east, the monster, Assyria, kept her oppressive foot upon the world.

But he must not think of these things now. His father was calling him, the faint name "Jeroboam!" rattling between hard sighs.

"Coming, Father!" he replied, wiping sweaty palms on his robe and entering the chamber, head bowed.

The priests stepped aside and Joash reached out a palsied hand, grasping his son by the shoulder and drawing his ear to his dry lips.

"Do you remember my instruction?" the king whispered.

"I do, my lord," Jeroboam answered, his own words choking him.

"Obey God and his prophets," the old man reiterated. "This is all that is required. And if you do this, you shall prosper."

Jeroboam chafed under the instruction. He could not enumerate the times Joash had said this. But bitterness against Elisha had wedged itself firmly between his soul and the Lord, and the thought of such obedience was repugnant.

"I shall, my father," he hedged.

Despite his frailty, the king discerned the hesitation.

"You strain at the bit," Joash rasped. "Warfare boils in your blood. But . . . ," the king insisted, drawing him closer yet, "learn from the ways of your father. First tear down the altars to Baal and Astarte, for this cleansing I never completed. And then turn your eyes to conquer the world. You shall not succeed until you do this. . . ."

Joash was failing. His breath came more heavily, and his words with greater effort.

Tears swam in Jeroboam's eyes. How could he do as his father wished when he had no faith?

Suddenly, Joash spoke his final word, his eyes flickering with a momentary light. "Elisha . . . ," he pleaded, his lips curling in a faint smile. And then his head fell back, his grip going limp in the hand of his son.

Jeroboam stood up and faced the priests who bowed to him now, chanting the release of Joash's soul and the ascent of the new monarch.

The young king eyed them scornfully, then proceeded to the balcony once again. Dreams of glory filled his mind, boring through his grief, and he viewed his realm with a lift of the chin.

Let no "holy man" interfere with him. He would bear with no prophet.

CHAPTER 2

It was a year for the rise and fall of monarchs. The king of Judah, just before the death of Joash, had been lowered from his position as ruler to the status of figurehead. By popular demand, after his defeat at the hands of Israel, his sixteen-year-old son, Uzziah, had taken actual command of the throne.

To Israel this was cause for leering laughter and scorning triumph. For Judah, it could mean nothing but improvement.

For Assyria, who usually watched the political wranglings of her numerous vassals with shrugging indifference, the deaths of provincial kings and the coronations of their successors were rarely of consequence. When one of her own kings died, however, and when one of her own sons replaced him, it was occasion for worldwide mourning and imperial pomp.

Adad-Nirari III, king of Nineveh, mon-

25

arch of Assyria, and Master of the Universe, was dead. Out from the palaces of Nineveh's most renowned patriarchs, from the glorious compound of royal heroes, two trains wended. The funeral procession was first, and thousands wept as it passed. For the departed king had restored Assyria's faded glory, making her again the power of the world, and bringing even Babylon to its knees. Egypt trembled, and all the earth — from the Tigris to the Nile, from the Gulf of Persia to the Great Western Sea — had bowed to Adad-Nirari.

Though their god, Asshur, rarely demanded human sacrifice, the occasion of a monarch's death necessitated it. The virgin chosen for the privilege would accompany him into the afterlife, as well as usher in the new kingdom.

And so the parade began, with black as its primary color, muted harps and cymbals mourning the passage of the old regime.

Upon its heels, however, came spectacle and color.

Shalmaneser IV, son of the departed, grasped his new position like a conquering hero. Having waged no wars and having won no military victories, he nonetheless chose to approach his coronation standing in a chariot, leading an immense marching army.

Past splendid temples to Asshur's cohorts — Ana, Baal, and Ea; Sin, the moon; Shamash, the sun; Ishtar, queen of stars; and Ramman, god of storm — he rode, past royal mansions lining the Khoser River, and toward the Covered Gate. The gods smiled on him as he proceeded, so he believed, and so did his enthused subjects.

At the gate the priests waited, overshadowed by the city's fifty-foot-high wall. There, to the blasts of trumpets, they would receive the virgin's life and the old king's soul, releasing it to the northern mountains from whence they believed mankind had descended. And at the same site, Shalmaneser would receive his crown.

The walled section of Nineveh was only three miles long, stretching beside the Tigris like a teardrop. But with its numerous suburbs it was enormous, well deserving to be called "the Great City."

Its conquered nations had other names for it, however: Nineveh the Bloody, and the Cruel. Assyria was notorious for merciless revenge. Nowhere in the annals of warfare could there be read more hideous or sadistic accounts of the treatment of enemies.

But such was the necessity of rule, Adad-Nirari had claimed. And Shalmaneser must expect to treat his continually restive colonies in like manner.

Babylon had never acquiesced to her own defeat. And Syria was always an upstart. Though Adad-Nirari had brought it about, the very fact that Syria had been weakened had allowed its little neighbor to the south, Israel, to rise up, expanding her borders considerably, and even taking courage to turn on her own sister, Judah.

Even now the dead emperor's words haunted Shalmaneser. "Beware the least likely foes," he had warned. "Let not the smallest rival escape your thumb. For small becomes great when the empire's eye is averted."

Shalmaneser, however, could not so much as recall the name of the new Israelite king. Why he should flash to mind amid this triumph, he could not imagine.

Intently the Assyrian prince turned his thoughts to the waiting crown. His strength lay in chariots, horses, and standing armies. Who could prevail against him?

His father's black procession circled past the priests of Asshur, offering up the virgin amid cries of lust and pain. And after the old man's soul had been received, the dark train retreated back along the Khoser River, toward the ancestral tombs.

The gleam of the crown fell across Shalmaneser's face as it was lifted in priestly hands above his head. A frenzied shout of exultation rose from the watching crowd as the world's new monarch received his diadem. And Shalmaneser ascended the throne, ready for glory greater than his father's.

CHAPTER

3

Jeroboam and Shalmaneser were more alike than not. Though most of their subjects had little reason to compare the two — one being Monarch of the World, and the other merely one of his many tributaries — there were those in Judah and Israel who considered their similarities important.

It took a keen observer and a future-minded man to heed such things; and it took spiritual perspective. But there were those in Jeroboam's realm, and in the sister province to the south, who were so gifted. They sat together in doorways and under grape arbors and in the gates of small towns, discussing these matters. They saw the ways of Shalmaneser and of Jeroboam, and they were alternately pleased and displeased.

Grateful they were that the eastern monarch had not, in his first years of rule, continued the military aggression of his father.

Though he had given every indication of planning to emulate Adad-Nirari, to this point he had focused on strengthening his occupying troops, rather than on conquest. And he was preoccupied with palatial pleasures rather than with imperial oppression.

When it came to Jeroboam's military reticence, however, sentiment was just the opposite. Those who still clung to the doctrine of the Promised Land wondered why the new king of Israel ignored his father's strides in territorial expansion. Surely Joash had paved an easy way. When his son did not immediately continue to chip away at Syria's southern borders, the zealous of the realm grew discontent. After all, Elisha's restriction on Joash surely did not apply to Jeroboam. There was no reason in prophecy why he could not strike against Damascus.

But like Shalmaneser, Israel's young king had been diverted from the strong intentions with which he had begun his career. The pomp and glamour of royalty had stolen his heart. He spent all his time indulging his senses, launching grand beautification projects in the capital, dallying in the most lavish merrymaking the nation had ever seen.

Where were the prophets this time? Was there no Elisha for Jeroboam? Such were the questions which troubled sober minds.

Amittai, the tentmaker of Gath-hepher, was one of those who questioned.

Sitting against the doorpost of his cottage, he wiped the sweat from his brow and ran a needle adeptly through thick layers of goat's hair fabric. Clicking his tongue, he shook his head, and continued conversing rapidly with two fellow townsmen. His mind was not on his work. It need not be, as after a lifetime in the business, he worked his designs without thought. His mind was miles to the south, in Samaria, and his heart was heavy with conviction.

"He spends our taxes to fortify the capital with a double wall," he mourned, "but he has not the protection of Jehovah!"

"Indeed," Machem said, nodding and stroking his own patriarchal beard. "The sanctuary of Beth-El, the most hallowed ground in Israel, has become a brothel!"

"And his noblemen grow fat on tribute!" Rezen added. "Utterly unscrupulous they are. While we live in hovels of unburned brick, they erect for themselves houses of hewn stone!"

"Meanwhile, Jeroboam lives in an ivory palace!" Amittai reminded them.

At this they all shook their heads again and looked sadly at the decrepit cottage that the tentmaker called home.

Jeroboam's citadel had become famous for its carved ivory, as he had imported the finest artisans from Egypt and Phoenicia to execute inlays for its walls and furnishings. The limestone dwelling, the glory of Israel, had always sported an extensive outer court and private pool, overseen by an impressive rectangular tower. But Jeroboam had enlarged the palace until it rivaled the homes of the greatest rulers on earth. And he filled it with loose feasting, relegating the practice of religion to mere ritual, allowing idols to occupy seats beside Jehovah.

"There may never again be such a time," Amittai grieved. "Assyria is moribund. The great Dog of the East lies sleeping, and no one in Israel makes a stir. We could advance, now, against Damascus. Against Hamath! But," he sighed wistfully, "we have a king of little heart."

Inside the cottage, a younger Hebrew listened in silence to the observations of the elders. He did women's work today, as he often did, and as someone in the household had to do, since his mother had passed away. But the talk of the respected men of Israel always stimulated him, making him long for action.

Though Amittai, his father, and fellows like Machem and Rezen might never earn a place in history and might not achieve fame in the world, they were holy men, he knew. Content with simplicity and the study of the law, they were decent and God-fearing, prone to see all things as from the hand of the Lord.

Kings of earth, they believed, were raised and lowered by Jehovah. Regardless of what deity a given monarch might serve, he had been enthroned by the Almighty, and could be overthrown at his will.

Shalmaneser was no exception. Nor had been Adad-Nirari. All events of history revolved around Israel and Judah, and were conducted under the watchful eye of El Shaddai, Adonai — God of the Hebrews, by whatever name he might be called.

If there was any understanding of the game the Holy One played with the nations, or of its ultimate goal, the understanding came through prophets.

Elisha had been the last. And now there was none.

The young man who overheard the political review stepped out from the house, wiping soapy hands on his tunic. Taking a place beside the elders, he sat cross-legged and quiet. A thousand questions he had, but he kept them to himself.

Everything about the youngster was dark and brooding. More often than not he blended into the shadows of his surroundings. Though he had a slender, agile strength that belied his stature, one might forget him easily upon first meeting — were it not for the luminescent gaze of his piercing blue eyes.

Because he was so often quiet, his father had named him Jonah. "Dove," the word implied, cloistered and unimposing.

Jonah remembered when, as a child, his attention had been drawn to a pale gray pigeon perched on his windowsill. "Some doves are gray," Amittai had explained, "and some white. But the eyes of each, whether dark or pale, are the most striking feature. And their quietness . . . their quietness is their strength, for it strains the ear and amplifies their song, when it comes."

Though Jonah was very young, and very quiet, his words, when he did speak, revealed a deep, contemplative spirit.

"During the days of David and Solomon, the Hebrew kingdom virtually engulfed Syria," the elder Machem was noting. "How can any Israelite king rest until those boundaries are reclaimed?"

"Perhaps," Jonah offered, "because the Hebrew kingdom is divided. Perhaps we will never be the same until we rejoin our sister province to the south."

The patriarchs squirmed uneasily at the suggestion.

"After all," Jonah continued, "the ten tribes of Israel *were* apostate when they rebelled against Judah."

"So we have been charged," Rezen chafed. "But there were good reasons for our rebellion. The taxation, the forced labor, and the military service of Judah were oppressive! Besides," he laughed, "you never were known for your conservatism. Why, sometimes I think you would embrace Nineveh herself, given half a chance!"

The younger man bristled. "You may not appreciate my tolerance for our southern brethren, though they *are* our fellow heirs with David himself. But you go too far when you accuse me of love for the Gentiles!" he objected. "My very loyalty to all Hebrews means I must oppose Nineveh!"

Amittai's old eyes sparkled. He was proud of his son's confrontive nature, and though they often disagreed politically, he loved a good argument. Today, however, Jonah would not satisfy his yearning for debate. Sidestepping other issues, he deferred to a far more important matter.

"I agree that Jeroboam is delinquent in matters of aggression," he acknowledged. "But were there a prophet just now in Israel, he would not confront the king with boundaries and warfare. He would face him squarely with our spiritual decline. What would it profit Israel if she sprawled across the world? Her heart is far from Jehovah, and so long as it is, she will always be small."

CHAPTER
4

Shalmaneser, king of Assyria, walked with
his ministers along Nineveh's northern wall
and strained his vision toward the distant
Ararat mountains. His father's colonizing
had always been west and south. His interest had never branched far east or into
the highlands of the north.

The mountains were the home of barbaric herdsmen, whose wealth lay in iron
and flint rather than gold and silver. No
great cities had they founded to pique the
lust of Assyria's covetous nature. But Adad-
Nirari would have been wise to keep an eye
on the back door of his kingdom. For while
he concentrated on westward expansion,
certain of the barbarian tribes plotted
against Nineveh.

The vicious and cunning mountain men
had been wise to await his demise. In
Shalmaneser they now saw a chink in
Assyria's armor. For years they had sent

38

scouting expeditions along Nineveh's borders. Recently, one such party had been detected, but when word reached the emperor, he had not been troubled.

Notorious in battle, utterly fearless, the barbarians were known for their love of risk. It would not be unusual for them to attack a walled city; but Shalmaneser took confidence in his armies.

As the monarch watched the highlands, he spied something flashing red on the crest of one hill. Nudging the fellow beside him, he said, "Call the prince."

At this the minister motioned to a fine-garmented lad and brought him forward.

Shalmaneser studied his young son. The boy shuffled restlessly and pulled away from his father's beckoning gesture, preferring to stay with his little sister, who had accompanied him on the outing. The king, with a flicker of displeasure, growled at him. "Look!" he commanded, pointing to the light along the hill. "Do you know what that is?"

The prince glared in the direction of his insistent finger. "Should I?" he quipped.

"If you desire to be a warrior, you should," Shalmaneser snarled. "That is the shine of the setting sun against a barbaric shield. There is a war party upon that hill!"

The boy's eyes grew wide. "Mountain men?" he marveled.

"Indeed," the monarch replied. "If you were emperor, what would you do?"

The lad was used to such tests. But he did not respond as Shalmaneser would have wished. "I could follow the example of my grandfather . . . or of my father," he offered, giving his sister a covert wink.

The king studied him with a gimlet eye. "Meaning what?" he asked suspiciously.

"I could obliterate the dogs before they lift a paw. Or," he said with a shrug, "I could do nothing."

Shalmaneser's face contorted. Raising a fist, he threatened to send the child sprawling, but then thought better of it.

Ashur-dan, the young prince of Assyria, merely watched with disdain as his father turned again to the northern mountains.

The king, seeing that the ghostly spies had departed, trembled.

CHAPTER
5

Jeroboam, king of Israel, reined his charge down the Samaritan highway. The buff stallion stamped and snorted as the rider directed its head toward the incline of Beth-El.

Incense poured in heaves from doorways of brothels along the road, and the horse resented the odor. Had he borne a spiritual sense, he would have also resented the aroma for what it represented: the decline of Israel.

The king had come to this most holy place to worship, his arrival unexpected. He had preferred it this way, as he wished to perform his religious duty quickly, avoid the intrusion of public applause, and be gone. But the moment he was recognized, with his train of officials, the town went wild.

Jeroboam was very popular with all but the most orthodox Hebrews. To the masses he was a well-balanced man, retaining the worship of Jehovah without shunning other deities.

The Beth-El sanctuary testified to his religious equanimity. The hallowed ground, where the patriarch, Abraham, had first erected an altar, had also been the resting place of the Ark of the Covenant after the escape from Egypt. Samuel the prophet had judged the Hebrew nation from this site. Under the munificence of Israel's first king, the shrine had been widened to include an idol of a golden calf, reminiscent of worship at Sinai. Then, under Ahab, altars to Baal and his consort, Astarte, had been erected.

To the liberal minded, Jeroboam's continuance of such practice was commendable. What better way to unify one's subjects than through open acceptance of all religions?

As Jeroboam rode up the avenue leading to the small temple atop the rise, the street was lined with spectators cheering, waving palms, and singing.

The handsome king nodded to them tolerantly, his shoulders thrown back and chin lifted. Behind rode a minister bearing a gilded bird cage. Two fine pigeons were perched within the swaying container, their round eyes alert to each step of the minister's horse. Jeroboam would sacrifice both birds this day: one to Jehovah and one to Baal.

The gold-leaf shrine glistened in the afternoon sun. It had been preserved in royal state at Jeroboam's insistence; and while a simple altar to Jehovah occupied the center, the left wing had been extended to accommodate a stone pillar to Baal and a bronze tree to Astarte — balancing out the golden calf, which occupied the right.

The people's applause grew louder as Jeroboam neared the hilltop. But suddenly a shuffle and a parting of the crowd nearest the shrine interrupted the proceedings.

"Come to Beth-El and sin!" someone was shouting.

All eyes turned toward the small porch of Jehovah's altar. There a peculiar figure had taken a stand, arms thrown back and face lifted toward heaven.

The king's party halted in the middle of the avenue and Jeroboam's eyes flashed angrily at the intruder.

"Thus saith the Lord!" the strange character was crying. "For three transgressions of Israel, and for four, I will not turn away the punishment thereof! You have sold the righteous for silver, and the poor for a pair of shoes!"

The king turned to his ministers, as if demanding that they do something, but they only stared at the eccentric preacher in wonder.

He was a windblown and dusty fellow, garbed in homespun, with wild, fiery eyes and a weathered countenance. His skin, his robes, and his long disheveled beard were all the color of the earth; and his gnarled staff, which he raised toward the sky, was worn shiny where his hand grasped it.

"You covet the very dust upon the head of the poor," he continued, "and turn aside the way of the meek!"

Jeroboam listened uneasily and spurred his horse a few steps toward the shrine, but the speaker did not pause.

"A man and his father share the same girl, to profane my holy name!" he cried, pointing to the porch where such brazen atrocities were performed. "Beside every altar they lay themselves down, drinking the wine of the damned in the house of Baal!"

The crowd, which had given its curious attention to this point, now murmured. Hostility escalated with the prophet's every word. "Did I not lead you out of Egypt?

44

saith the Lord. Did I not raise up your sons as prophets? But you gave them wine to drink and said, 'Prophesy not!' "

Now the king dismounted, confronting the rustic messenger with a hateful frown. "Tell us your name!" he commanded. "And be gone!"

The preacher stood eye to eye with the monarch and did not move. "I am Amos, a shepherd of Tekoa," he replied. "I am your prophet for this hour."

Jeroboam's face grew pale, though he tried to hide his fear behind a leering smile. "Prophet?" He laughed. "I have reigned a full decade without a prophet. Is this an afterthought on Jehovah's part?"

The crowd was delighted with the king's wit, and laughed with him. But Amos was unimpressed.

"A shepherd . . . of Tekoa, you say?" the king baited him. "Could God Almighty find no prophet in *Israel?* Did he have to dredge one up out of *Judah* to send me word?"

Amos faced him squarely. "David was a shepherd of Judah, O King," he reminded him. "The Lord roars from Zion, and utters his voice from Jerusalem. When the shepherds mourn, even the top of Carmel withers! *For you blaspheme the purposes of God!*"

Jeroboam peered down his nose at the Judean pilgrim. "I think you are a madman and no prophet," he snarled. Then, mounting his horse again, he turned to leave.

"Behold," Amos cried after him, his face full of storm and his wild hair flying, "I am pressed under you as a cart that is full of sheaves, saith the Lord! Therefore, flight shall perish from the swift, and the strong shall grow weak. The mighty shall not deliver himself, neither shall the archer stand in that day!"

Jeroboam nodded to his ministers and rode away, his horse's hooves kicking up dust behind him.

The fellow who kept the dove cage was bewildered, and leaning down from his own mount, set the container upon the porch.

Amos bent over and opened the cage door, releasing the pigeons in a flurry of gray and white feathers. Then, studying the king's departure, the prophet shook his staff skyward again and warned, "Neither shall he that rides the horse deliver himself! And he that is courageous shall flee away naked in that day!"

CHAPTER
6

That day . . . that *day!*" The words echoed in Jeroboam's head, sending shivers down his spine.

The prophet had not specified what would transpire upon "that day," but no one could mistake the portent of his words. There was, according to his admonition, a day of vengeance coming upon Israel, upon the king.

Jeroboam lay his head back against the soft lap of his concubine, Marna. She was, for this evening, the chosen one of his harem. Tomorrow it might be another, but for several weeks, Marna had won his fancy. She caressed his temples with oiled fingertips, running her hands seductively over his shoulders, as a warm breeze wafted up the valley and through his balcony window. The girl's voice was like sun-warmed honey. "The moon peeks over the Great Sea," she said. "It is a clear night."

The king made no comment, his thoughts farther away than the moon.

"Your brow is furrowed, my lord," Marna noted at last. "What troubles you?"

Jeroboam turned over on his large pillow and let her knead the tense muscles of his back. "Nothing you would understand," he assured her.

Marna had heard about the incident at Beth-El. She wondered whether to inquire about it, or feign innocence. Knowing that her position as his recent favorite was tenuous, she kept her questions to herself, and tried to distract her master with a piece of candied fruit.

"Apricots from Gilead," she crooned. "Fresh today. . . ."

The king sat up and sighed, looking past her. He walked to a narrow sofa and reclined, leaving no room beside him. His fingers traced circles on the lounge's ivory inlays, going round and round like his thoughts.

Marna observed him in frustration, and at last rose quietly to leave, gathering her oils and perfumes.

"Where are you going?" Jeroboam halted her.

"Why, I assumed you wished to be alone," she answered weakly.

"You assume too much," he snapped, glaring unhappily at her. And then, his face softening, he spoke more kindly. "Do not assume I wish you to leave. Always assume the opposite."

He held out a solicitous hand, and Marna's fearful eyes grew warm again.

Sidling to him, she stepped behind the couch and began once more to work her magic on his shoulders.

Marna was new to Jeroboam's chambers. He had first discovered her at Beth-El: a prostitute of Astarte, dark and sultry, like the heathered hills of Phoenicia, where she was born. "Like Jezebel," he had told himself. "No wonder Ahab had been unable to resist the princess of Tyre."

That was how it had begun, he knew — the worship of Baal in Israel. Once Ahab had married the foreign woman, he had been at a loss to keep her religion beyond his borders. Now Jeroboam understood how such a thing could happen. Though Marna was only one of his concubines, he thought of her too often. Had she insisted, he would have permitted her to worship Astarte on the grounds of his very palace.

To this point, she had not asked. Such presumption would not have occurred to her. She was, after all, not a wife, but barely more than a well-established harlot.

His lip curled as she massaged his back. When it came to Marna, his heart was a riddle. He could as easily send her into destitution as raise her to glory. For now he preferred to take all she could offer, and leave it at that.

But, between thoughts of fleshly pleasure, the prophet's words haunted him.

Suddenly, he again forgot the woman whom he had just summoned to his side. Standing, he left her supple grasp, and exited the room, down the narrow stairway to his courtyard. Passing the guards who watched his private quarters, he went beyond the court wall, and paced the broad porch overlooking the highway to Esdraelon.

He did not know in what way calamity could strike. He had done his best to fortify his hilltop city. Commanding the trade route to the coast, it was an easily defended site. As Marna had noted, even the Mediterranean was visible from the three-hundred-foot mount, and valleys on all sides provided ample warning of any approaching foe.

Why, were Nineveh itself to attack, the city of Samaria could prevail, he assured himself.

No, whoever this mad shepherd thought he was, he had no power to subdue Jeroboam.

The king listened to the rush of valley breeze that swept across his walls. From inside the courts of his noblemen laughter and music echoed, mixing in pleasant refrain with the wind. He would not join the party tonight. But he would enjoy the sounds of revelry.

Turning, he found that Marna had followed him from his room. She leaned against the archway to his porch, moonlight catching her white tunic in a soft glow. He smiled at the sight of her in the shadows. Then he walked to her, slipping his arm about her waist.

As he led her back to his chamber his heart throbbed to the sounds of the desert and the lilt of a distant flute.

There was no Elisha to trouble him, no Amos. Samaria was secure behind stone walls, and so was the king.

CHAPTER
7

Jonah, the tentmaker's son, rushed home from market, thrusting two great bags of unspun goat's hair onto the hearth floor. He barely had time now to prepare supper. Amittai would be displeased.

The old tentmaker entered the cottage door, rubbing his knees. All day he had pursued the sewing of a giant tarpaulin. So broad was the material, he had been forced to work on it in a kneeling position, stretching his arms before him and applying the needle to endless stretches of seam. He was ready to eat a good meal and to examine the purchases that his son had made at the bazaar.

"Did the wool come in from Shechem?" he inquired, already seeing his answer in the large sacks upon the floor.

"Right there," Jonah replied, pointing to the pile as he busied himself over the cook fire.

Amittai perceived that his son's thoughts were far away. "You were gone a long while today," he mused. "What happened this time?"

Jonah's father knew it was difficult for the lad to step out of the house or go into the streets without being distracted. It was difficult for a young man to stay indoors so much, and to be burdened with "women's work."

The old tailor knelt once again and fumbled through the burlap wrappers. "Heavy and coarse — good . . . ," he muttered. "Good wool. . . ."

Then, peering up at his son, who stirred a thick broth in an iron pot, he sighed.

"So, tell me. What detained you?"

Jonah glanced at his father sideways. Then, unable to contain his news, he stood up and tossed his ladle onto a nearby table.

"Father, a prophet has come to Israel!"

Amittai's eyes narrowed. He shook his head and chuckled low.

"Yes, Father! A prophet. At Beth-El!"

The tentmaker sensed the strength of Jonah's conviction, and though he doubted, he could not help but inquire further.

"Who told you this?" he asked.

"It is all over the village! Everyone speaks of it! The seer is a shepherd . . . from Judah."

This last fact was added softly, and with hesitation. As was to be expected, it generated a strong reaction.

"Judah?" Amittai cried. "Why would a Judean be messenger to Israel? No, my son, even Jehovah could bring no good from such an arrangement."

Jonah sighed and cast his eyes to the ceiling. "Never will you see beyond our doorstep!" he protested. "Father, Judah is as much the Lord's as Israel. Why, David himself was a Judean!"

Amittai shook his head, but made no rebuttal. "Very well," he nodded at last. "You say he preached at Beth-El?"

"Indeed! And daily since then he has moved north, approaching Samaria."

The elder, despite his national prejudice, would hear more. "And what does he preach? Does he speak against the ivory palaces, the oppressors of the poor?"

"He does, Father. He preaches . . . calamity."

Jonah turned to the small window that looked from Amittai's cottage past the village walls, and south toward the capital.

Should the prophet ever speak there, he would hear him firsthand. He would feel the citadel of Jeroboam tremble when the time came.

"A lion roars! Who will not fear?"
The voice was becoming familiar in Israel. Today it challenged the worshipers at Gilgal — especially the wealthy, overfed women who had come down from Samaria to pay tithes at the temple there. The message was the same as that given at Beth-El, but amplified now to contain more specific judgments.

All about the holy place they had stood since morning — the plump, painted wives of Jeroboam's noblemen, lisping and giggling together, spending small fortunes in the market on cosmetics, perfumes, and trinkets.

When it came to religious observances, it hardly concerned any of them whether they sacrificed to Baal or Jehovah, and it mattered little how much they deposited in the coffers, which fed the shrine's keepers. Gilgal was merely a place to flaunt one's extravagance, survey the latest fashions, and catch up on courtly gossip.

When at noon their social competition was interrupted, they were unprepared to think seriously about anything.

"Hear this word, you cows of Samaria!" Amos cried. "You who crush the needy, who say to your husbands, 'Fetch wine, that we may drink!'"

Charcoaled eyes and berry-stained faces turned to spy the source of the offense. When they found him, the road-worn pilgrim, they laughed among themselves. But he continued.

"The Lord God has sworn by his holiness: Behold, the days are coming upon you when they will take you away with meat hooks, and the last of you with harpoons!"

Did he refer to them? they wondered. Wanton lips drew into pouts, and scorning chins turned upward.

"Come to Gilgal and transgress! Bring your sacrifices every morning, and your tithes every three days," the shepherd mocked them. "For so you love to do, O Israel! But I will return unto you cleanness of teeth, and lack of bread in all your houses. I will withhold rain so there is no harvest! Plague, pestilence, and war are your due. Scorching, mildew, and the devouring worm!"

The women clung together, no longer laughing. Despite the man's rude appearance, he spoke with authority. And they were horrified.

Amos had drawn close to the altars of the holy place as he had spoken, his wild eyes flashing retribution. Now he seemed content to leave. And raising his staff, he shook it ominously in their gaudy faces.

"Prepare to meet your God!" he warned.

Then, as quietly as he had come, he went away.

The "cows of Samaria" were silent, some laying their gifts on the altar before they departed, but most forgetting the task.

Their husbands must hear of this. Surely they would know what to do.

CHAPTER
8

While the words of Amos circulated through the land, and as the king of Israel pondered the prophet's obscure references to future devastation, Shalmaneser, king of Assyria, endured the threat of imminent assault.

The barbarians of Ararat were playing a game with Shalmaneser, trying to wear him down in mind and spirit. He would have known how to proceed against Babylon or Egypt. He had seen his father strike out, and he had studied war himself.

But how to fight an enemy so elusive as the mountain dwellers, he could not fathom. To this point they had not shown themselves to be an army. They slinked around the edges of Nineveh, like cats spying out a distant bird's nest. The barbarians would be a formidable foe, should they ever gather together. But, were they to do so, he could at least strike a blow. When they approached in small bands, padding along the horizon like panthers, Shalmaneser could do nothing but wait.

It was the waiting that was so wearing . . . and the realization that they *knew* it compounded his frustration.

Doubtless they were aware that his ministers also prowled about him, daily inquiring as to his plans. When was he going to *do* something? they kept asking. Did he have a strategy? Were the troops prepared?

But how could one prepare for such an unknown enemy? Yes, the walls were fortified. The guards had been posted for weeks, and all squadrons stood on alert.

It was his son, however, who troubled him the most. More than his ministers; more than the barbarians themselves.

The young prince, Ashur-dan, seemed to delight in his father's ambivalent stance. "Send war parties toward the hills. Let them scout out the tribes and pick them off," he would insist.

"But that would weaken our command of the city," Shalmaneser would argue. "Should the barbarians invade, we would not be as strong with the units dispersed."

"Then, maintain them here," the lad would say, nodding.

"And wait like a stunned gazelle for the leaping wolf?" the king would object.

Ashur-dan would not reply. He had appeased his own need for challenge at the expense of his father. And the ministers shook their heads.

Truly, Shalmaneser had no plan. The one who had expected to follow the military path blazed by his ancestors was immobilized.

All this was to the benefit of the mountaineers. Their strategy was daily gaining them ground.

The year the barbarians first struck was the last year of Shalmaneser's reign, and the first of Ashur-dan's rise to power.

When Ninevites would someday look back over the brief decade of Shalmaneser's rule, it would seem an aborted thing. For he had prompted great hope at the beginning — promise of continued Assyrian might. But he had never performed, dallying instead in comforts purchased by previous generations' dying soldiers.

The night his military challenge did arise, he was no match for it. He was drunk upon a harlot's bed when the enemy scaled Nineveh's walls.

Two days before, they had attacked Arbela, over fifty miles to the south. That should have been warning enough. But even then the emperor had not mobilized his forces. He had stationed them, instead, inside the gates of the capital, believing they would be better used there than in defending a neighbor.

The barbarians had steadily encircled the imperial hub, until all means of escape were cut off.

When the disgusted ministers had been unable to rouse their lord from sleep, they had quickly installed Ashur-dan as regent-king, and the lad had made his first decision as commander-in-chief of the royal forces.

It had not been too late to retrieve a victory.

Shalmaneser, rising in the middle of the night with an aching head and wrenching stomach, had stumbled to his watchtower to find a full-scale war raging beyond Nineveh's walls. Though his army subdued and routed the enemy, he was humiliated by his own ineptitude. His death at his own hands, upon his own sword, would not be recorded in the kingly chronicles. Only the fact that he had been replaced by a boy would be remembered for long.

And the city would busy itself, under Ashur-dan's direction, preparing for yet other visitations from the northern mountains.

CHAPTER
9

It mattered little to Jeroboam what was developing in Nineveh. Assyrian colonies were aware of the repeated barbaric invasions into the empire's eastern reaches. But they were little affected. So long as Nineveh, imperial Dog of the Tigris, kept its oppressive paw at a distance, no vassal country much cared what struggles the capital endured.

Each little kingdom beneath the Assyrian banner had its own concerns to handle. Emotionally there was little allegiance to the emperor. Obeisance was a political expedient, wrung from less-than-willing hearts.

Not did it much matter to Ashur-dan that the tiny realm of Israel was being invaded by its own marauders, an enemy not of flesh and blood, against whom no arms could be taken. If word trickled to the Ninevite palace that famine and drought had struck northern Palestine, the emperor only hoped it would not slow the flow of tribute from that region. It certainly was not his policy to aid a suffering satellite, unless it would benefit him directly.

King Jeroboam was alone with the worries of his own state.

Today he rode through the Israelite countryside, peering over the low walls of hamlets and burgs with Marna, his established mistress, close behind. All along the route of his royal entourage, the sick and the hungry stood, hands outstretched over the stone partitions that shielded their towns from the roadway.

Jeroboam was not an utterly hard or unfeeling man. If he had "oppressed the poor," as the prophet had insisted, it had not been a conscious or willful oppression. It had been because he was sheltered within his palace, little touched by the lot of commoners.

So this was what he had been hearing of — the ravaging of want and destitution that reportedly surrounded his gilded halls and carpeted aisles. Yes, there was disease and horror in the land. For five years now the conditions had worsened — ever since the shepherd from Tekoa, the pauper-prophet from Judah, had risen.

Jeroboam could almost reason that Amos was to blame. Israel had been at the height of prosperity when the ominous voice of the doom-crier had first thundered at Beth-El.

But the king knew better. Logic told him no simple sheep-prodder could have brought his nation to its knees.

Amos had not yet come to Israel's capital, however. There surely was hope for the nation as long as the scourges of nature and infections of the air lingered only upon her villages and hovels.

Marna stirred impatiently beneath the canopy of her high cab as it swayed lazily upon the back of a great dromedary. The woman peeked with disdain from between silken curtains, covering her nose against the stench of the masses below. After five years as Jeroboam's favorite, she had nearly forgotten her own origins. It distressed her to be reminded in this way.

Unlike her childhood heroine, Jezebel — the first Phoenician to take the throne alongside a Hebrew king — Marna had come from a less than regal station. Her father was but a poor tanner of Sidon — a profession not scorned in her native country as it was in Israel, but a lowly calling, nonetheless. As a young girl she had been accustomed to the putrid animal carcasses over which her father labored, to the scavenging for hides, and to the skinning which was part of his livelihood. She had known squalor.

But she had been redeemed from her destitute life-style by her own beauty — raised to a place of Phoenician honor as a prostitute of Astarte. Her prospects had been upward-looking ever since, and she dreamed now of rising even higher. Marna would be queen of Palestine's northern realm, she was determined.

And like Jezebel, who had persecuted the prophet Elijah, she would take arms against any soothsayer who threatened her blossoming hopes. If Amos took comfort in Jeroboam's passivity, he would be wise to watch the seat beside the throne. For it would be from Marna that his demise would issue forth.

All this the priestess of Astarte, the salvaged harlot, fantasized as she rode behind her paramour. One step up from concubine, one step away from wife, she watched Jeroboam's back as he silently surveyed his stricken subjects. Did he pity them? she wondered. He should spend his time on greater matters. Did he fear the shepherd of Judah? He need not do so.

Closing her curtains against the pleading masses, Marna leaned her head upon an embroidered pillow and shut her eyes. Let Amos never set foot inside the capital, she sneered privately. Or he would not live long past that act.

CHAPTER
10

A hot wind parched the broad avenue leading from the gate of Samaria, Israel's capital, to the hilltop palace. All along the dry gutters folk stood still and quiet, watching Amos as he made his way boldly toward the citadel.

The quaint Judean was not so out of place in his appearance as he once would have been. Almost everyone in the capital was garbed in dust these days, and little grandeur remained to distinguish the kingdom's hub from the ravaged villages round about.

Huge decorative cisterns beside the road, once an architectural pride of the city, were hollow now, and children played atop them, casting pebbles into their dark interiors. When they laughed at the empty reverberations, interrupting the silence, fathers scowled and mothers ran to them, dragging them back into the crowd.

Had the prophet been able to see past the throng to the doorfronts of many homes, he might have noted that some people had removed the family idols from their doorsteps. Even now, as he passed certain abodes, women quickly draped the small guardian *baals,* which stood watch at their portals. Black were the shrouds and morbid, indicative of shame and perhaps repentance.

Amos did not think much of these token acts. His heart thundered against the generations of evil that had finally brought the judgment of God upon the people. What were a few shrouds in view of the great sin of this city? What were token gestures at this late date? The ruins of the temple to Baal, built by Ahab and broken down by Jehu, could still be seen on the terrace of Samaria's mount. Such destruction had not changed hearts for long. Always the seeds of paganism lay in the ground of Israel, ready to sprout under fertile conditions.

From the crowd, one dust-smudged face watched the prophet's advance with more than typical interest. When Jonah had heard that Amos was due to arrive at the capital, he had arranged with his father to be gone from home for a few days.

Trekking the thirty miles from Gath-hepher, he had arrived in Samaria just minutes before the anticipated visit. Now he peered over the heads of the city dwellers, his breathing tight.

As the shepherd-sage neared the palace gate, a flash of color drew the crowd's attention to a small balcony, high beside the royal watchtower. Jeroboam, followed closely by his scarlet-garbed mistress, had suddenly shown himself beneath unfurled banners. Contrasting gaudily with the simple herdsman, he held the gaze of the congregation until Amos raised his staff.

"If a trumpet is blown in a city, will not the people tremble?" the familiar voice cried. A thrill of whispers then an awed hush ran through the throng.

"If calamity strikes a city, has not the Lord done it?" he demanded.

His visage was full of lightning as he spoke. No one dared challenge his words.

Shaking his massive stick toward the tower, he continued vehemently: "Proclaim on the citadels of Ashdod and on the walls of Egypt, saying, Assemble yourselves on the mountains of Samaria! See the great tumults within her, the oppressions in her midst! They do not know how to do what is right, declares the Lord, these who hoard up violence and devastation in their palaces!"

Had such accusations been heralded here a few months previous, the messenger would have been stoned in the street. Following as they did on the heels of famine and fear, the words fell on ready ears. And the public, which had always supported the popular king, today murmured agreement, turning doubtful eyes toward their monarch.

Indeed, more than doubt was manifested. There were those who encouraged revolution. They were few, to be sure, but their numbers were growing. And even among those who still loyally maintained allegiance to the crown, there was restlessness and agitation.

Jeroboam, despite a calculated show of confidence, fidgeted with a tassle on one sleeve. He easily read the mood of his subjects.

Rarely did he make a public appearance. Whenever he had in the past, he was greeted by enthusiasm unequaled in Israel's history. The pall of quiet that greeted his entrance this afternoon spoke louder than all the cheers of previous praise.

Yet he knew he must not betray his trepidation to the masses. He would at least question the one who trespassed on his glory. Lifting his noble chin, he raised a hand, and Amos paused in his castigations.

"We know you claim to be a prophet," the king began.

The audience jostled for a clear view of the challenge.

"Tell us, O Chosen One," Jeroboam sneered, "do you also take credit for the sufferings of my people?"

The listeners might have laughed at his wit. They would have done so in days gone by. But now they could not appreciate his hollow sparring, and heads shook as discontent mounted.

"No, Your Majesty," Amos replied. "For the desolation of your subjects, *you* may take full honor!"

The crowd roared approval, feeling the thrill of vengeance.

But Amos had not forgotten their part in the matter. Turning to the audience, he declared, "Woe to all through whom offense has come! The city that w: thousand strong will have only a hun left, and the one that went forth a hunc strong will have remaining only ten!"

Every man stood corrected, and every

woman blushed. There was no defense against his judgment, as each heart reviewed itself.

Marna seethed with anger, and reading Jeroboam's paralysis, nudged him impatiently. Stepping up behind him, she whispered something in his ear, and he studied her uncertainly.

Trying to reflect his regal station, he cleared his throat and drew closer to the balcony rail. "Well spoken, Amos," he faltered. "But, then, tell us what lies ahead."

The sarcastic edge with which he had meant to tinge his voice was somehow lost, and the mistress at his elbow glared at him with contempt.

Amos cared nothing for their private war. Pursuing the king's question straightaway, he replied, "As it was with Sodom and Gomorrah, so shall it be with you! Prepare to meet your God, O Israel!"

Suddenly another figure appeared at the archway to the elevated porch. Those who could see him quickly identified him as the king's high priest, Amaziah. It was to Marna, however, that he leaned in covert conversation.

Jeroboam did not see their interchange, as he stood, white knuckled, at the balustrade. When he turned a quick glance for his lady's further suggestion, he found her gone.

The hallway guards saw her depart into a conference room with the holy man. They could not have guessed at their plot. And Jeroboam would not have wished to overhear it.

CHAPTER
11

Five years later there was an altar to Astarte in the courtyard of Samaria's palace, and a new queen had been installed beside the throne.

Of course, another queen had been removed for this to be accomplished. But it would not be the first time Jeroboam had arbitrarily lowered another to satisfy his own whims. The fact that his maneuver was illegal troubled him little. These days, Jeroboam's decisions rarely took into consideration the proprieties of Hebrew tradition.

It seemed that the more matters deteriorated in his country, the more his heart was hardened. The voice of Amos continued to plague him, as the shepherd made repeated appearances near the palace. But Jeroboam did not repent.

How much his path was of his own conjuring, and how much it was influenced by

Marna, was a perpetual source of speculation among his subjects.

Tonight, the "harlot-queen," as she had been dubbed by her critics, stood before the foreign altar, performing the oblations required of her sect. Dressed in the sheerest of fabrics, which hung now only upon her hips, she had stepped into a brass basin; and as she meditated upon the Phoenician goddess, a chambermaid caressed her legs and bare torso with a splashing mixture of aloes and oils.

No man was supposed to be allowed within the little grotto that she had long ago designated as her place of worship. But it was often the case that those walking along the court gallery were privy to glimpses of her. And she did not object as strongly as she might.

Jeroboam had been informed of such indiscretions; but though his heart was pricked, he had never raised a finger to correct her.

It was even rumored that at times she summoned the high priest, Amaziah, to her bathing quarters. Though she was always garbed by the time he arrived, the scents of the bath and the suggestion of what he had missed always titillated him.

When he was called to such encounters,

he knew what the topic of conversation would be. What was Amos up to these days? she would always ask. Where was he preaching? And what were his predictions? Then they would speculate as to how they might best silence him.

The king would never go against the shepherd, they knew. Though his dreams were troubled by the rustic's message, and though month by month his mental state grew more unsteady with the prophet's proddings, Jeroboam feared the Judean.

Tonight, as Amaziah made his way to Marna's grotto, his eyes fell once again upon the peculiar decor leading to the sanctum. Though the "holy place" was a fabrication, occupying one corner of the inner court, it was intended to give the illusion of a wilderness haunt. Small palms, buckets of reeds, and bullrushes set into man-made ponds lined the aisle approaching the bathing cloister. Linen lotus blossoms created by palace seamstresses, and diminutive statues of bulls, lions, and sphinxes, along with bowered shrines to Isis and Horus gave an Egyptian flair. But the spirit of Astarte, goddess of love, predominated in small murals and carvings of courtly romance.

Amaziah, though no fan of Amos, nonetheless retained enough Hebrew scruples to question the merit of such "high art." He never gazed upon the love scenes too closely, as they affected him more than he dared admit.

The chambermaid was just coiffing Marna's dark tresses when Amaziah arrived. He bowed low as he passed beneath the den's trellis, and, bidden to sit awhile, tried to keep his mind on business despite the dizzying effect of the lair's steamy perfume.

"Amos preaches near Nazareth," he answered the queen's first question. "And he says, 'The virgin of Israel has fallen and shall not rise again. . . .' "

Marna sighed and flicked her hand impatiently. "Yes, yes, is there nothing new?"

The priest's hesitation told her that indeed there was something new, and that he did not wish to relay it. Flashing dark, disapproving eyes, she drew him out with a sigh. "Go on, Holiness! Surely by now you do not think I could grow squeamish over his vile forecasts. What does he say?"

Amaziah's gaze lingered over the fine bed upon which the lady lounged, and over the gilded cup from which she drank. The heady aroma of the cave tickled his nostrils, and he shuddered.

"He says . . . he says . . . and these are *his* words, madam, not mine . . ."

"Go on, go on!" She scowled.

"He says, 'Those who recline on beds of ivory, and sprawl on their couches . . . who eat lambs from the flock . . . who improvise to the sound of the harp and drink wine from ornamented cups . . .'"

Marna studied her goblet and set it down gingerly, but said nothing. So Amaziah continued.

"Who anoint themselves with the finest oils . . . ," he whispered.

"Yes, speak up, man," she ordered. "What did you say?"

"Who anoint themselves with the finest oils," he repeated, his eyes tearing.

Marna's face reddened. Angrily she turned to her maid. "Leave us!" she growled, and the chagrined servant complied.

"Shall I proceed, madam?" the priest asked, his middle-aged heart so stirred by her distress that he could not discern compassion from erotic desire.

"Are you mad? Of course, you must proceed!" she shouted. "What does Amos predict shall happen to me?"

Amaziah stammered. "O madam, I

would not take his torments person-
ally. . . ."

"And just how *should* they be taken?" she
huffed, rising from her bed and pacing the
little grotto. "Now, I insist that you give
me the full report!"

Closing his eyes, the priest recited the
fearful message from heart, knowing that it
would gain him no favors with his mistress.
" 'I loathe the arrogance of Israel, says the
Lord. And I detest its citadels. Therefore, I
will deliver up the city and all it contains.
For, behold . . .' "

He looked at Marna, the pronouncement sticking in his throat.

" 'For, behold,' " he repeated, " 'I will
raise up a nation against you, and they will
afflict you from the entrance of Hamath to
the brook of Arabah.' "

The queen's breath came sharply.
Grilling the man with a hateful expression,
she spat, "There is more, is there not? You
withhold the worst of it!"

Casting his gaze to the floor, Amaziah
nodded sadly. "He adds, 'Thus says the
Lord, I will then rise up against the house
of Jeroboam with the sword. . . .' "

This was not said in a whisper. The
priest did not wish to repeat it.

Marna trembled. Gathering her thin

robe tight, until it clung filmlike to her damp skin, she stood.

"Amos has spoken his final time against the king," she swore, her voice catlike and low. "I shall sleep on this and speak further with you tomorrow. "

Now Amaziah trembled. He did not like her decisive tone, but as he rose to leave, bowing low again and backing out through the trellis, he dared not survey her face. She, like all she worshiped, reminded him of his guilt, and of the path of betrayal that he had long ago chosen.

CHAPTER
12

Jonah sat up with a start. It was midnight in Gath-hepher. Moonlight streamed through the cottage window and onto the floor past his pallet. He strained his ears to determine what had wakened him at this odd hour. He had had no unsettling dream, nor could he hear any sound but that of the soft breeze, which usually blew over the evening village.

As he grew more alert, however, he realized that he was covered with a dewy sweat, and that his hands trembled.

"What is it, Lord?" he found himself asking. Then, feeling somewhat foolish, he leaned once more upon his pillow and tried to rest.

But, again, the moment sleep overtook him, he lurched awake, and spoke to the air.

"Yes, Lord. Your servant hears," he cried.

Covering his mouth, he peered toward the fire where his father lay. To his relief the old tentmaker was undisturbed, snoring peacefully despite his son's peculiar outburst.

Jonah, however, knew it was not his night for sleep. Rising, he stepped to the firepit and threw a small log upon the embers. As the flames leaped to life, they cast strange shadows along the opposite wall. Jonah shook his head with a laugh. "Come, now," he muttered firmly, "your imagination races."

But he was certain of what he saw. Yes — there in silhouette, suspended against a high corner of the room — it seemed the prophet Amos stood before the altar of Beth-El.

Suddenly, for no reason Jonah could determine, a sense of certain danger filled him.

"Amos, you must not go to Beth-El!" he wished to cry.

Though he had not spoken aloud this time, the phantom in the corner responded.

"It is the will of God," came the unearthly reply.

Jonah's skin goose-prickled. But his urgency to protect the prophet was all-consuming.

The tentmaker's son stood frozen to the hearth for a long time. It was not until Amittai began to rouse that Jonah realized dawn had broken the night. The flames of the fire had long since returned to smoldering, and the apparition on the ceiling had vanished.

The old man sat up and scrutinized his son.

"Did you not sleep, my boy?" he inquired. "You do not look well."

Jonah rubbed his eyes and ran trembling fingers through his disheveled hair. Not knowing how to answer, he hunched down upon his heels, his face ashen as the floor of the cooling firepit.

"I do not know if I dreamed, or if I woke . . . ," he stammered.

Amittai leaned forward in curiosity. "Something troubles you. Can you speak of it?"

"A voice . . . a man . . ."

The elder studied his awestruck countenance, then made his own deduction.

"A man, or . . . more than a man?" the tentmaker proposed.

Jonah looked at his father in surprise. "You know, then," he whispered.

Amittai rose stiffly from his pallet and gazed quietly down upon the youngster.

"Always I have known this day would come," he confessed. "Always I have known you were a special one. I sense that your hour has arrived."

Jonah had never heard his father speak this way. He did not even know how to question him. He had no understanding of the night vision, and no strength to analyze his strange new feelings.

"I lack direction, Papa," he groaned. "I saw Amos, Papa. Amos was in this room!"

"And did he call you?"

"Not really. . . ."

"Do you wish to go to him?"

"More than life itself!" he cried.

Amittai stepped close and offered his hand, lifting the young man to his feet. "Find your cloak and put on your sandals, my son," he urged. "Then find Amos, and God be with you."

CHAPTER
13

Amaziah, the high priest, had a wife and family. It was easy to forget this when he was thrown into Marna's company. But the reality confronted him whenever he returned home to Beth-El. And a pleasant reality it was.

His headquarters were stationed at that holy place. Though he spent more time at Jeroboam's palace, his family fulfilling his duties in his absence, he was always more comfortable at the site of the ancient shrine.

Today his plump and comely wife and two daughters worked at polishing the golden calf beneath the right awning of the little temple. Normally, he would have watched their activities with contented satisfaction. But this afternoon he was burdened with word from the palace, a letter from the king received in response to his own correspondence.

Only days before, he had, at Marna's insistence, sent a message to Jeroboam informing him of Amos's doings.

The fact that he had stretched the truth, coloring the prophet as an insurrectionist, haunted him now. He tried to excuse it on the basis that the queen had commissioned the lie. But that part of him that still revered Jehovah squirmed uneasily at the betrayal.

He turned the parchment of the king's reply over and over in sweaty hands. The monarch had not ordered Amos's death; for this he was grateful. But he had commanded that Amaziah see to it that the shepherd never speak again in Israel.

At the thought of even that trespass, the high priest shuddered. He knew too much about the ways of God to take such a prospect lightly. He had not lost all his conscience to paganism, though he dearly wished he might. To be a man divided was a fearsome thing.

A gleam of setting sun flashed across the golden calf and reflected off Amaziah's face. He shielded his eyes against the glare and found a tear resting on his cheek. Wiping it quickly away, he was glad his wife had not perceived his struggle.

Rising, he walked to the curtained meditation room behind Jehovah's altar — not to pray, but to hide himself.

Twenty-six miles away, in his own chamber, Jeroboam read and reread the message received just days before from Amaziah, and with it a copy of his response.

"Amos has conspired against you in the midst of the house of Israel," the accusation claimed. "The land is unable to endure all his words. For thus Amos says, 'Jeroboam will die by the sword and Israel will certainly go from its land into exile.'"

The king sighed heavily and went to his balcony, pacing to and fro like a frustrated lion. What choice had he but to order the shepherd's silence? Indeed, he reasoned, it was highly likely that Amos was in league with those who, for months, had whispered revolution in the country.

But could a prophet's vision be altered, just because he ceased to speak? In truth, even were the pilgrim preacher put to death, he had already made his pronouncements, and their portent had given Jeroboam many sleepless nights.

Sometimes the monarch felt he was losing his mind. Nothing brought him peace anymore. His banquets, his women, and his wine only exposed his emptiness. Marna churned up his agony as often as she appeased his guilt. No longer did her fleshly offerings placate the gnawing hunger of his soul.

The queen did not come much to his chamber these days. Too often he was uncommunicative when she did try to win him. Too frequently she found a storm upon his face, and a furrowed brow. Sometimes his withdrawn silence and his sharp rebuffs frightened her. And rarely did he call for her company of his own accord.

All this Marna laid at Amos's feet.

Tonight, as she passed down the corridor beyond Jeroboam's room, she hesitated and glanced inside, hoping vainly that she might be invited in. As usual, the king was oblivious, standing for long minutes upon his elevated porch, gazing vacantly across Samaria.

They would share nothing this evening — neither the nectars of love nor the Mediterranean moon. And Marna would place her head upon a lonely pillow, her only solace her private dreams of Amos's overthrow.

CHAPTER
14

What Jonah would most remember of the second and last time he saw Amos was the prophet's cloak — the mantle that spoke of the open road, of wilderness, and of mission.

Jonah had departed Gath-hepher with his heart in conflict. Tears had dimmed his eyes as he passed beneath the dawn-lit gate of the little city and pondered when he would again see his father. But the call of adventure was hot in his blood, and the search for the unknown lured him on.

What design Jehovah had laid for him, he could not imagine. Were he to think on it too deeply, he might have doubted his night vision, and even turned back. But the dream's unspoken summons could not be denied. Though neither Amos nor God had specifically told him to leave home, or to go seek the prophet, he knew in his heart he was meant to do so.

Nor could he imagine what part he

would play in the shepherd's ministry. He only knew that with each thought of the Judean sage, an overwhelming sense of danger prodded him to make haste for Beth-El.

Though he had seen the preacher only once before, he could not have missed him in a crowd of thousands. The day he arrived at Beth-El, just hours after leaving his native village, he located the man with ease, drawn like flint to a target.

Not that Amos allowed anyone to overlook him. Once again the prophet stood upon the temple steps, decrying the oppressions of Israel and the sins of her people.

Jonah pressed through the throng until he came to the front edge, very near the porch. He stood and studied the seer, with longing in his piercing blue eyes. He desired to reach out and touch him, even to grasp the hem of his garment. "Be careful, Master," he would have urged. "Your enemies are all about. . . ."

In fact, however, the entire congregation appeared to be on Amos's side. For the famine and plague that had ravaged the country had not spared its holiest sites. Not even the mount of Abraham's first sacrifice nor the seat of Samuel's judgment had been immune to God's wrath.

The streets of Beth-El groaned with disease. Malnourished babes rummaged after withered breasts, and folk grew old before their time.

When would Jeroboam turn the nation about? they all demanded.

Yet, the people themselves still bowed the knee to Baal.

It was not until Amaziah and a half dozen temple guards entered the stage behind Amos, however, that Jonah could clearly identify the enemy.

In the prophet's ten years of preaching, he had never been confronted by the high priest. It was apparent that, though Amos's entire ministry opposed him, Amaziah feared dealing with him directly.

But the royal edict must be delivered.

The priest could have approached the task with more confidence, had he been infused only with Marna's venom and his own pride. But he still bore in his blood a vestige of reverence for God — a tarnished pearl of conscience. Could he but crush that pearl to a powder, he would be stronger.

As it was, he trembled. Though men bearing spears and shields stood with him, and though he carried the unfurled scroll of Jeroboam's injunction, his hands shook.

The crowd read his apprehension, and watched him closely, wondering what challenge he would bring. The prophet, seeing their distraction, turned to face his accuser.

"Amos, son of Judah, native of Tekoa," the priest interrupted, "I bring word from the palace of Samaria."

Amaziah's firm voice belied his trepidation, giving him an air of confidence beyond himself.

The people murmured. A message from the king? Might Jeroboam at last be taking their plight to heart? Perhaps Amaziah's trembling heralded a change of policy regarding the state religion. Let the monarch only lead, and they would follow. For they were ready to depart from Baal.

But they overestimated Jeroboam's spiritual sense.

Avoiding the shepherd's gaze, the priest read from the tasseled scroll. "Word has come to me, O Amos of Judah, that Israel can no longer bear your voice in its streets and villages. You have been charged with conspiracy against my throne and government, and stand accused of stirring up the people to fear the future. Therefore, I, Jeroboam, king of Israel, command that you go, O seer! Flee away to the land of Judah, and there eat bread and there do your prophesying!"

At this point the priest dared seek the face of Amos, and gathering all his strength, read the finale with mounting conviction.

"But no longer prophesy at Beth-El," the order concluded, "for it is a sanctuary of the king and a royal residence."

The pilgrim was quiet as Amaziah rolled up the epistle, handing it to the guards. When the priest turned to him again, waiting for a reply, there was no movement or sound of breathing among the crowd.

Jonah, studying the temple's armed men, grew tense, sensing that Amos dared not resist.

But the Judean evinced no fear. Speaking softly, he at last answered the edict; and as he did so, Amaziah's back drew up rigid and straight.

"I was not born a prophet," the shepherd began, "nor am I the son of a prophet. I am only a herdsman and a farmer of sycamore figs. But the Lord took me from following the flock and said to me, 'Go prophesy to my people Israel.'"

Of all the defenses the man could have framed, this was the last his accuser wished to hear. The preacher could have challenged the distorted charges. He could have claimed right to counsel or the testimony of the public on his behalf. But to refer to his sacred call, or to the hand of God upon his head, was to present the irrefutable. Amaziah argued from the flesh and Amos from the spirit.

The priest fumbled for a retort.

But the shepherd was not finished. The familiar storm flashing from his eyes, he challenged his accuser.

"Now hear the word of the Lord!" he cried, pointing a fearsome finger in the priest's face. "You are saying, 'You shall not prophesy against Israel, nor shall you preach against the house of Isaac.' Therefore, says the Lord, Your wife will become a harlot in the city; your sons and your daughters will fall by the sword; your land will be parceled up by a measuring line; and you yourself will die upon foreign soil!"

The cry of female voices could be heard beyond the tapestry separating Amaziah's family quarters from the temple porch. The high priest, enraged, lunged for the man of Tekoa, nearly knocking him to the ground.

A great deal of movement followed, too

fast for Jonah to reconstruct. That the guards went to their master's aid, and that Jonah himself was suddenly at Amos's side, would be well remembered.

And that somehow the tentmaker's son found himself standing between the priest and the prophet, was a certainty. He would not know later how his presence had defended the preacher against the spears and swords of Beth-El. He would only recall that, suddenly, the guards had fallen back, freeing Amos to grasp Jonah by the arm and lead him out through the crowd.

As the prophet left the temple, he continued to deliver his warnings, insisting over and over, against the wailing of the throng, "Israel will certainly go from its own land into exile! *Exile! Exile!*"

And as the shepherd made his final appeal, dragging the youngster through the press, he was removing his famous cloak, the one that had earned him the dubious title of "pauper-prophet."

When he reached the edge of town, with crowds pursuing him as far as the gate, he took Jonah to a grove of sycamores bordering the village entrance.

In the company of a remnant who were determined to be with him to the end, Amos turned Jonah's bewildered face toward his own. Holding the wide-eyed one firmly by the jaw, he studied his countenance for a long moment. Then, nodding, he lifted the notorious mantle in rugged hands, and draped it over Jonah's shoulders.

"Woe to the distinguished men of the foremost nations," he declared, plumbing the Hebrew's gaze prophetically, "to whom the house of Israel comes!"

Then, looking once more upon the gate of his enemies, the seer simply turned down the south road, disappearing toward Judah.

Jonah was left beneath the sycamores, his head spinning and his tongue cleaving to the roof of his mouth. The faithful few who had followed Amos from the city surveyed the tentmaker's son with wonder.

But the young Israelite feared to contemplate the meaning of the cloak.

PART TWO

DISOBEDIENCE

But Jonah rose up to flee . . . from the presence of the Lord. . . .

JONAH 1:3

CHAPTER
1

It was very quiet in Israel this evening. Too quiet for Jeroboam.

He should have been happy, Marna pouted. Surely tonight, of all nights, he should have welcomed her presence.

At least she had been admitted to his chamber. As she sat now upon his carpet, her head resting against his velvet ottoman, she ran her finger over the veins of his sandaled foot, sighing repeatedly.

"The noblemen's wives desire a party," she said at last, breaking the oppressive silence.

Jeroboam did not reply.

"There is a festive mood about the palace, my lord. Do you not feel it?" she spurred him.

But the king could not sympathize. Something within him had died. Pressing his fists to his temples, he closed his eyes.

Marna studied him, incredulous. This

very day his enemy had been overthrown. Amos, thorn of his soul, had been routed — sent back to the wilds of Judea, never to trouble the province again. Could Jeroboam not appreciate all she had done for him?

Sitting back, the queen put her hands upon her hips and scowled angrily at her husband.

"By the gods, Jeroboam!" she cried. "One would almost think you miss the madman! Can you not be grateful for a little peace?"

The king pushed her away with his toe and leaned forward with a bitter face. Gesturing toward the window, he demanded, "Peace? Is there peace in a land when its people are dying? The silence of Samaria is not the silence of contentment!"

Standing on shaky legs, he paced before the aperture, eyeing his city with an aching heart. "O Lord Jehovah, for the cry of a suckling child!" he pleaded. Then, turning on Marna, he growled, "When did you last hear a newborn wailing? There are no children born these days; had you noticed? There is only death. Only mourning in the streets!"

The woman, still sitting beside the couch, clutched a pillow to her breast. She had never seen her lover in such a state. She feared his every move.

Now and then he paused, leaning his head toward the balcony, as if listening for something, someone. Then, frustrated, he would steady himself and hold his hands again to his temples.

"They throb, Marna!" he would cry. "My ears . . . they throb with the silence."

Perhaps if she soothed him, she thought. Rising, she approached and drew him close, placing a cool hand upon his forehead. "Let me ease the tension in your neck, my lord. Remember the way I used to rub these muscles . . . just so . . . ?" she whispered.

But the king had little patience for such things. Jerking away, he avoided her touch.

"It is Amos you desire," she murmured, her face falling.

Jeroboam's countenance altered at the mention of the prophet's name. Marna could not interpret the expression, whether it was of wonder or fear. But she knew she had spoken the truth.

Gathering up her robe, which she had laid upon his couch, the queen sighed again. When she left the chamber, Jeroboam made no objection.

He had gone to his porch once more, straining his ears through the vacant air, craving the voice of God.

CHAPTER 2

Jeroboam stood at the door to his father's chamber, which had been locked ever since the old monarch's death. The butler who kept the key did not question the opening of the sanctuary after all these years. But he must have wondered, as did all who lived with the son of Joash, why the king behaved so strangely of late.

He simply wished to be alone, he told the custodian. And after waiting for a candlestand to be lit, he motioned the fellow to leave, shutting the door in his bewildered face.

The room was musty and cold, seeming still to smell of death and mourning. Jeroboam drew back the heavy curtains, allowing daylight to filter past the memories trapped within.

He could not account for this compulsion to enter the place. But the instant he was alone he found himself communing with his long-departed sire. Had anyone been present he would have blushed at this foolishness. However, it mattered not in private that his breath came quickly or that his heart raced. No one but he felt the sweat upon his brow or the palsy in his hands.

Clearly he heard again his father's last words, and as he relived those moments he knew why he had come here. It was necessary to his own sanity that he reconstruct Joash's exhortation. Though shame filled him at the reminder of his own failure, he knew he must face it squarely.

"No, my father," he whispered, "I have not fulfilled your commission. Altars to Baal still stand in Israel. The faithless flourish, and the people die like sheep without a shepherd."

Jeroboam's face was hot with the confession. And as they had so often of late, his ears burned for the comfort of guidance.

"There is no prophet, now, my father," he cried, his voice broken with sobs. "No Elisha . . . no Amos!"

Slumping to his knees, he grasped the bedstead whereon the previous king had lain, and he wept like a child. "The borders of the country have not moved," he admitted. "The land withers, while it could have grown."

All his years of idle folly flashed before him, and his inability to turn them back settled over him like a shroud.

It seemed he could see Joash's face; and overlaid, the faces of all the prophets who had ever prophesied, and all the judges who had ever judged.

It was too late to recall Amos to the land. Once a king declared an edict, it was irreversible. The Judean was gone forever, and Jeroboam felt impotent to save his people with no seer at his side.

"I too am but a sheep," he mourned, rocking back and forth upon his knees.

The flames of the candlestand suddenly wavered in peculiar fashion, as though something had passed through them. And following this, a sudden scuffle was heard in the courtyard below.

Rising, Jeroboam walked to the portico upon which he had waited the night of his father's death. Straining his eyes toward the palace gate, he watched as two guards tried to turn someone away.

He could not identify the stranger who demanded entrance. But something about him was familiar.

The king's heart stirred, his pulse quickening. "Let him in!" he called to the determined sentinels. "Send him to me now!"

Within moments the visitor stood at the doorway to Joash's chamber, and Jeroboam hastened to admit him.

The king need not ask Jonah's purpose. The instant he recognized the cloak of Amos on his back, he knew his calling.

Falling before him, the ruler clutched at his ankles, and the tentmaker's son placed his young hands upon the monarch's head.

Had Jonah thought long on the situation, he might have trembled. But somehow it seemed natural to be here. Somehow it seemed right that Jeroboam should greet him in this way.

For God was with him, and the mantle of Amos fit him well.

CHAPTER
3

The year Jonah entered the palace of Samaria was the year young Ashur-dan, king of Assyria, began ruling without the overseeing counselors necessary in his adolescent period. And he was determined to exercise his full authority with a show of force that would regain for Nineveh its dignity after nearly a decade of barbaric invasions.

He began by moving fresh forces into the Cappadocian merchant colonies along the Black Sea. Then he strengthened the trade routes to the commercial tributaries of Anatolia. When these acts drew the resistance of Haran, which lay along his path, he sacked that great city-state with military fervor unseen since his grandfather's reign.

The poundings of the mountain men, which had weakened the empire's northern flank for nine years, were henceforth not so formidable to Nineveh's morale. Successes in other areas drew the focus off those defeats, and gave the capital hope for the future.

In such strategy there was strength and weakness. While the Ninevites badly needed a sense of power, there was danger in averting attention from the foe who continued to play along the realm's upper edges. It was apparent to those who studied such matters that Ashur-dan's punitive raids against his underlings were merely a cover for inability to master the mountain barbarians.

And his inflated boasting, too, seemed but a cover.

Today he rode with his sister, Kisha, through the market of Nineveh, dictating to his scribe in an open chariot. As was typical of the royal line, Ashur-dan was of average height, but powerfully built, and like most Assyrian males, he was dark, with a prominent nose, luxurious, bushy hair and a thick, wavy beard. But unlike his fellows, he was not of a cheerful disposition, and was not given to mirth and feasting.

Had he been visible to the commoners of the market, and not hidden behind a large umbrella held by a slave, he would have attracted the gaze of every female in the place. For Ashur-dan was famous for his good looks, a gift for which he seemed to have little use.

Since childhood, he had lived for only one thing: the throne and its power. Departing from his father's ways, he had never been one to dally at parties or encourage the frivolities of the noble class.

Building an imperial reputation was his goal. And blatant propaganda, along with his recent military thrusts, was part of his program.

Just now his scribe took down the words to an inscription, to be carved beneath every statue to the emperor throughout the realm. "Let it read, 'Mighty King, King of the Universe . . . ,'" Ashur-dan suggested, "'the King without rival, the Autocrat, the Powerful One . . .'" He paused and thought a moment, then smiled. "Yes, 'the Powerful One of the four regions of the world. . . .'"

Kisha watched in silence as the scribe copied the phrases exactly, pressing his stylus into the small clay tablet which fit neatly into the palm of his hand. And she shuddered as in a burst of inspiration Ashur-dan added, "'. . . who shatters the might of the princes of the whole world, who has smashed all his foes as pots!'"

The scribe nodded obediently, and

wisely hid the knowledge that, almost to the word, such an inscription had been devoted to a previous king. Surely Ashurdan knew this, but the servant would be foolhardy to remind him; so he merely waited, assuming there might be more to come.

"That will do," Ashur-dan sniffed, and the scribe climbed out of the vehicle, bowing quickly, and then running for the palace.

The king had come out today for the ride and for the air. He was not in the market to buy, nor was he here to offer up a morning or evening sacrifice, to lay a gift of wine, milk, honey, or cakes at the feet of the numerous statues to his ancestors, which adorned Nineveh's square.

Many of his predecessors had achieved deification centuries after their demise. He intended to qualify for such immortality. Reading the numerous plaques upon the bases of the sculptures, his heart burned with envy.

The tablets were riddled with the only written language of the Assyrians, wedge-shaped cuneiform impressions reserved for monumental purposes only.

It was appropriate that hymns and poems to gods and kings should be inscribed in clay. Assyrians were, after all, the "people of the soil," everything from their houses to their pottery being the product of river bottoms and dunes of sand. Though limestone, alabaster, and marble were abundant, the citizens of the Tigris were proud of their link to the land, lauding it in legend and song.

Inscriptions to Ashurnasirpal II and to another ancestor, Shalmaneser III, especially provoked Ashur-dan's jealousy. Of the first, great praise was recorded concerning his exploits into the westland. "He washed his weapons in the Great Sea," it was chronicled, "and received tribute from the coastal cities of Arvad, Byblos, Tyre, and Sidon." Of the other, his son and successor, it was reported that he continued the tradition, invading Syria, marching through a coalition of twelve kings, and taking revenue from Phoenicia and Israel.

How little Ashur-dan had yet accomplished! Should he blame the barbarians or his own father's weak example?

Passing beneath the shadows of the statue-lined Avenue of Kings, the young monarch blushed. Lovely Kisha, his sister, observed his frustration, and read the heaviness of his spirit with a helpless sigh. Snapping his fingers, the emperor ordered his slave to lower the umbrella a bit further. And as he slumped back into his seat, the princess reached for his hand, her delicate features clouded with concern.

Meanwhile, Ashur-dan's jaunt through the market had created a stir among his devoted subjects. They thought he was wonderful, as they bowed before his chariot and whispered excitedly to one another.

But he did not acknowledge them.

The driver whipped the horses to go faster, sensing the master's discomfort. Ashur-dan wished only to go home. Perhaps, in the quiet of the palace, some inspiration could come, some plan that would catapult him into the star-strewn galaxy of the immortals, and capture for him a place in chiseled clay.

CHAPTER 4

Jonah had been lodged in the finest guest quarters of the Samaritan palace since the evening he had arrived. Jeroboam was determined that *this* holy man be treated well; and so, with nearly feverish persistence, the king had overseen preparations for the newcomer's comfort.

The next morning, the ruler's zeal had not cooled, but seemed to have grown even more energetic. And when he summoned Jonah early to his throne room, the young stranger was greeted by a breathless host.

Jeroboam was pacing the narrow carpet, which ran the length of the room. Rubbing his hands together, he seemed eager to set matters out, and did not wait for Jonah to speak before he began.

"I know, I know. . . ." He nodded. "You will tell me that I must rid the land of idolatry and of vice. Well, this I will do! Indeed, I have already sent forth a party of soldiers to tear down the high places and demolish the *baals* of my people."

He did not even look in the newcomer's direction before he continued. "Yes, yes, I know you are surprised. But I sent them out before sunrise, to show you I intend to obey!"

Of course, "surprise" was an understatement. All that had transpired in Jonah's life since the vision in his father's house had been like a dream — and a very strange dream, indeed. Now, here he stood, in a seer's cloak, beneath a royal roof, and before the king of Israel.

He was being catered to as a spokesman for Jehovah, when he had hardly so much as read the scriptures in the humble synagogue of his native village.

Jeroboam interpreted his silence as evidence of his holy station, and grew more emphatic in efforts to win his approval. "All morning I have been calculating how best to rid the country of sin," the king went on. "I can think of a hundred ways, but all are bloody!" he cried. "Would Jehovah wish me to purge the land by blood?"

Suddenly, Jeroboam was confronting the Chosen One. Jonah knew he was expected to speak. Had the youngster thought heavily on his own inadequacies, he would have fled the room. But, as though the words issued from another, he found his mouth uttering a peculiar thing, and he listened to himself as though to a stranger's voice.

"The Lord does not delight in blood and sacrifice," he replied. "But a contrite heart is his reward. You do well to tear down the houses of Baal, and of his lady, Astarte. But if you would serve Jehovah fully, you must rid yourself of Jezebel."

Jeroboam no longer paced the room. The instant Jonah spoke, he was riveted to him. And when the summary injunction was given, the king's whole body grew rigid.

His face pale, he stammered, "M-Marna? You speak of my wife?"

"I do," Jonah affirmed.

The king's gaze fell to the floor, and large tears rose to cloud it. For a long time he said nothing; and then, at last, shoulders slumped, he nodded again.

"In my deepest heart I knew you would demand this," he whispered. "Is there no other way?"

"None," the preacher declared.

With a sigh, Jeroboam turned for his high-backed throne and sank into it in utter dejection. Memories of his first months with the Phoenician woman stabbed him like burning goads — their forbidden pleasures riddled with regret and shame. It almost relieved him to think of ending it now.

He lifted sad eyes to the prophet. "And if I do this . . . , will my kingdom prosper?"

"Assyria itself will tremble before you!" Jonah asserted.

The monarch lurched forward, incredulous, and the young seer himself could barely believe he had promised such a thing.

But the words had not been his own, he knew.

Suddenly the king scrutinized him, as if truly seeing him for the first time, marveling at his simplicity, yet humbled by his luminescent gaze.

"Nothing but your eyes astounds me," he noted. "And the cloak of Amos upon your back." His tone was heavy with awe, and he reached out a hesitant hand. "I have not asked your name, my friend, or from whence you hail."

The preacher stepped forward. "I am called Jonah, son of Amittai of Gath-hepher. I was not born a prophet, nor am I the son of a prophet," he replied. His voice quivered now, and again he listened to it as to the voice of a stranger. "But I have received the commission of God," he asserted, "and will be his spokesman for this hour."

CHAPTER
5

It was inevitable that, though Jehovah did not require it, blood would be shed during the purge of Israel.

It began at Beth-El.

When Amaziah, the high priest, defied the soldiers sent to tear down the shrine of the golden calf and the house of Baal, his own house was ransacked, his sons and daughters hauled into the street and slain before the wailing citizens. His comely wife, too, was wrenched, crying, from her husband's arms and ordered never again to enter the temple residence.

Amaziah himself, despite his position as the nation's religious leader, was thrust into a waiting wagon, and carried away, with no word concerning his destination or his fate.

Ahead, however, along the same road that his vehicle followed, another wagon traveled from Samaria. It was an even cruder carriage, no more than a cart equipped with a cage of rugged branches and drawn by an ass. Its passenger, whose tear-streaked face stared through the bars in angry disbelief, was Marna, Jeroboam's queen.

She knew where she was headed — back to Phoenicia, to her father's tannery, and likely to her previous life of prostitution.

There had been no reasoning with the king. She had not even been allowed to see him after the guards invaded her room, binding her and ushering her from the palace. No explanation had been necessary as she was escorted past the dismantled ruins of her bower to Astarte, the little sanctuary that her husband once had permitted.

As she rode along Israel's famine-ravaged countryside, surveying its villages and squalid farms, she did not hide behind silk curtains or recline atop a canopied dromedary, as she once had done. This time, *she* was the object of scorn to all who saw her. They pelted her cart with small stones, and she became the target of spittle and curses.

She clutched at the shoulder of her gown where the rude guards had torn it, and she stared out from her cage in horror. All along the roadside were the smashed remains of household gods, thousands of little *baals* and their *baalath* consorts, willingly deposited there or forcibly taken from the homes of village folk at Jeroboam's command.

Even now, up the highway, she could see a half dozen horsemen wielding clubs and large hammers against a row of the sculptured figures. Slender, long-haired Baals crumbled beside bosomy Astartes, and with them lay fragments of Melkart, lord of the sun; Eshmun, god of the life force; and Reshef, the lightning deity. Sacred poles and stone pillars were scattered in disarray, and holy trees lay in splinters among them. Leveled altars and pillared halls scarred the hillsides and man-made "high places," testimony to Jeroboam's determination to serve Jehovah.

Replacing the sacrifice of animals and sacramental sex in the streets of Israel were mourning and loud lament, women garbed in black, faces covered, and old men sitting beside the road in sackcloth. Little children sat with them, and at their mothers' instruction, threw dust upon their own heads, and wept like adults.

As the queen rode past the demolition crew, she shut her eyes tight. But refusal to acknowledge the men did not conceal her own identity. Their vindictive laughter burned in her ears, until the sound of another wagon on the empty highway caught her attention.

The soldiers' scoffing was even more raucous as the cart of Amaziah drew up behind the queen. And the two prisoners stared at each other in speechless humiliation.

"A fit pair for Phoenicia!" one of the horsemen bellowed. "At least they'll have each other in their exile!"

The troops roared heartily at this, sparring with the silent captives as they were carried by.

Amaziah stared straight ahead, his face ashen. So, Phoenicia was his destiny. His skin crawled. Who would he be in that heathen land? At least in Israel his Baalism had been an ecumenical art. In the country of its origin, he would be nothing more than a religious hybrid, a spiritual oddity.

Marna flashed hateful eyes upon him, boring through his attempt to ignore her. And when he finally looked her way, she leaned her face through the bars and spat.

Wiping the saliva from his sleeve, Amaziah winced.

Whatever lay ahead, he knew he could descend no farther than this. His fall was complete.

CHAPTER
6

Jonah was becoming accustomed to the luxuries of palace life.

He had lived with Jeroboam three months, while the last vestiges of paganism were being routed from Israel. And as the king had gone beyond all expectation in conforming to Jehovah's demands, the young man from Gath-hepher had warmed to him, almost as though the ruler were an elder brother.

Indeed, Jeroboam encouraged his intimacy, calling him to dine with him, to sit at his fire in the evenings, and to ride with him on expeditions to see how Israel was rising to its feet. As much as Jonah missed Amittai and the elders of his village, he found his station in Samaria much to his liking.

"Did you know that Solomon raised doves as messenger birds?" the king asked one night.

"I have heard this." Jonah nodded.

"You are like that to me, much as your name implies you should be," Jeroboam said, smiling and offering the prophet a finger cake. Then, surveying the flames of his chamber fire, he added, "A messenger of God to me. . . ."

Jonah perceived the king's gratitude, and felt a blush rise to his face. "I have done very little to this point," he confessed. "I only carry the banner of Amos — and rather quietly at that."

The monarch laughed softly. "True. You are a gentle one. But were I to cross you . . ."

At this Jeroboam tossed a faggot onto the fire.

Jonah shook his head. "You project your own fears of Yahweh onto me. I have no power to make or break you," he objected.

"Ha!" Jeroboam shrugged, looking the prophet square in the eye. "Elisha broke my father. Tell me he did not!"

"He did not," Jonah replied without a pause. "Your father was his own undoing. And even at that, God blessed him."

The king reflected on this a long time, and as his gaze wandered through the lights and shadows of the fire, Jonah sensed he struggled with his own destiny.

Drawing near and peering into the regal face, the seer surmised, "You know what lies ahead."

"I suppose I do," Jeroboam whispered.

"Let me hear it from your own lips," the preacher demanded.

The ruler drew his shoulders back, headstrong. "*You* are the prophet!" he insisted. "Do not ask me to do your work!"

But the instant Jeroboam posed this challenge, he was ashamed. "Forgive me," he pleaded. "I had no right. . . ."

"Prophecy is not always the domain of the seers, O King," Jonah corrected him. "Sometimes it is simply the product of wisdom. And I believe that all your sufferings have taught you much." Then, rising from the hearth, the young guide continued, "Nevertheless, because you wish to hear it straight from God, I will reveal the contents of your own heart, and confirm to you the leading you already sense."

Directing Jeroboam, with a sweep of his hand, to consider the land which lay beyond the palace, he leaned forward with an intent face, his voice full of conviction and manly vigor.

"From the entrance of Hamath," he said, "to the Sea of Arabah . . ." His arms spread wide, indicating the farthest reaches, north and south, which had once formed the nation of the Hebrews. Then he reminded Jeroboam of the obvious implications. "As Joshua first determined, and as David and Solomon established, so must the boundaries of the kingdom be renewed."

The ruler's eyes grew round with awe. To accomplish this meant he must go against Israel's northern neighbor, Syria, and to reconstruct the kingdom meant also that he must go south and east against Ammon and Moab.

"But what of Judah?" he hedged. "Where is their stake in all this?"

Jonah leaned back, not at all surprised that Jeroboam should inquire thus. Indeed, for Israel to establish the original borders there would have to be involvement with her southern sister. The kingdom, after all, had originally been united, and reconstruction necessarily implied joint effort.

The prophet could see by his lord's sour expression that such a prospect pleased him not at all.

But for now, the matter was premature.

"Look to yourself and your place in the will of God," Jonah warned. "Do not concern yourself with your brethren."

Jeroboam sighed, his head spinning. "Perhaps there is more to do in Israel.

More altars to Baal . . . more sin to overcome. . . ."

Jonah smiled, empathizing with his friend's hesitance. "You have done well, Your Majesty. Do not look back. The will of the Lord is always toward the future."

Then, standing, he took the king by the shoulders and delved deep into his fearful eyes.

"The time has come," he declared, "to rebuild the nation of God."

CHAPTER
7

When Jeroboam went against Israel's northern neighbor, Syria, he would begin where his father had left off — at its capital, Damascus. And when he went against Damascus, he would also be going against Nineveh and the Emperor of the World — not only politically, but soldier to soldier and sword to sword.

In Ashur-dan's quest for military successes, he never expected the ignominious nation of Israel to be his greatest challenge. But within months of his determination to win a place among the conquerors of Assyrian lore, the little satellite demanded his attention.

Jeroboam, whose father had been bold enough to raid southern Syria and to turn on his sister, Judah, was suddenly, unaccountably, venturing into neighboring regions.

While the emperor had paid little heed

to the western colony when it had suffered under famine and plague, he was now taking notice indeed.

First Jeroboam marched against the Ammonites and Moabites, east of Jordan, moving the Hebrew tribes who once had owned those territories into their original homelands. Then in an unprecedented stab at political peacemaking, he somehow gained the favor of his perpetual rival, Uzziah of Judah, and engaged his aid in pushing the limits of Palestine south to the Gulf of Arabah.

Once all Trans-Jordan had been recaptured, from Gilead to Edom, Jeroboam turned his sights north, to the snowy heights of Mt. Hermon and the Abana River Valley — to its jewellike footstool, Damascus.

And once he did this, Nineveh, the Dog of the Tigris, roused from its slumber.

What went on within the Jordan region troubled Ashur-dan little. Borders and kingdoms might change hands over and over within that sector without provoking the concern of Assyrian leaders. But if a Palestinian state began to reach beyond the parcel linked by the sluggish Jordan, eastern rulers had reason to look twice — especially where Syria was concerned.

Damascus was too valuable to be winked at.

It was early morning when Jeroboam and his army first set foot along the Abana. The famed dews of Hermon still lay upon the river's grassy slopes, and the hooves of the soldiers' horses left a path of green between broad sweeps of silver as they entered the valley.

Damascus, radiant under the Syrian sun, begged for a conqueror. Jeroboam lifted his chin and filled his lungs with the sweet breath of the mountain range that framed the city. He turned to Jonah, who sat beside him in a small canopied chariot.

"My father was afraid of this place." He smiled, his own mighty steed stomping, impatient for battle. "Why do I feel so strong?"

Jonah nodded his understanding, confirming what the king already knew. "Jehovah is with you," the prophet explained. "You have sensed it and seen it for months. Damascus is no more powerful than the armies you have already subdued. No army is more powerful than any other in the sight of God."

"Not even the hordes of the Tigris?" Jeroboam marveled. "We know very well

129

that Ashur-dan may meet us here."

He referred to the fast-traveled news that troops in Assyrian garb had been spied along the highway south of Haran only days before. Every soldier in the Hebrew ranks was prepared for the eventuality that more than Damascenes awaited them.

"Not all the empires of earth can prevail against the hordes of heaven," the prophet reminded him. Then, surveying the plain upon which Israel glimpsed the coveted land, Jonah said, "Were our eyes only opened, we would see the hosts of God encamped about us, ready to do battle this day."

Jeroboam leaned down and placed a warm hand on the preacher's slender shoulder. "You are a worthy companion," he declared. "Stay beside me until the hour comes."

This Jonah was pleased to do, and even when the monarch lifted his lance, giving the shout and charging toward Damascus with his valiant troops, the prophet would stay upon the plain.

God had shown him what the outcome would be, and he must not miss the witness of it.

Damascus had been a troublesome area

for the empire to manage long before Jeroboam's time. Even during the reign of Ashur-dan's grandfather, the city-state had slipped from beneath Assyrian control, and had been retrieved only at great cost.

With Jeroboam's recent record of military successes, the emperor could not take lightly any threat he made.

But as Ashur-dan stood today upon the walls of Damascus, alongside its sovereign, more than the threat of Israel weighed his mind. He had told no one among his allies, not even his own officers, that he had received word of yet another barbarian invasion.

He was used to such reports, but this one had an untimely sting, for the mountaineers chipped away at the upper limits of Syria, the land he sought now to defend in its southern sector.

Though he wore a brave face before his comrades, his heart was shrinking. The irony of his dilemma was more than personal. For not only was his hope of immortality in peril; his empire itself seemed suddenly to be at odds with the universe.

CHAPTER
8

Jonah waited with Jeroboam's ministers beyond the southern gate of Damascus, a safe distance from the fray, as Israel stormed the immense walls of the city.

Never had he been near a war zone. Never had the tentmaker's son seen the smoke and leaping fire of a city under siege, or heard the cries of grown men at their deaths.

As a lad he had been raised on tales of Joshua and Gideon. He had heard of the unseen armies of God who had aided the Hebrews at Dothan and Jericho. David had been a mighty warrior, and so had Saul. But these names lived in legend, and no longer in flesh. What he saw before him was as tangible as flint and iron, as terrible as blood.

For three days and nights the battle roared, and Jonah caught rest between shrieks of fear and shouts of glory. From the beginning, Israel had met with uncanny success. But the prophet had known this would happen.

Though the Israelites were greatly outnumbered by the Damascenes — who, aided by Nineveh, could have routed the ranks of an Egyptian pharaoh — each Israeli arrow seemed to find its mark, and every spear its appointed target.

On the third night, Jeroboam sent for Jonah to join him at the headquarters tent, boldly erected within plain view of the city's tallest watchtower. Donning the cloak of Amos, reserved for the most hallowed occasions, he went to meet the king.

From the grassy slopes where his friend had left him, the preacher crossed a level field amazingly free of slain Hebrew soldiers. Though some had lost their lives before the might of Damascus, they were a small minority. If there were other Hebrew losses, they would be found inside the walls, testimonies to Israel's valiance.

As he made his way to the tent, he was also aware that the sounds of war had moved toward the city center; and, even at that, they were strangely muted.

When he arrived at Jeroboam's post, he found the king in a lively mood.

"The jewel of Hermon is ours!" the

monarch cried, greeting him with a warm handclasp. "Damascus will be Israel's by morning!"

"I surmised as much," Jonah said, smiling.

"The troops even now surround Ben-Hadad's citadel, at the core of the city. They will storm it tonight — the palace that my father never even saw!"

Then, grasping Jonah by the arm, Jeroboam bade him walk up along the wall.

A shiver of awe ran through the young man's body as he, who had known little beyond a small village in his life, looked down from the precipitous height of Damascus's evacuated ramparts. Indeed, the Hebrew losses, though wondrously few, had occurred inside the gate and not upon the field. More than the height made Jonah dizzy as he surveyed the bloody corpses of both armies strewn about the streets below.

From the top of the wall, one could not discern to which army any fallen soldier belonged. And their anonymity strangely haunted the man of God.

But Jeroboam was speaking again, and Jonah marked the confidence with which he made his forecast.

Pointing to the distant palace of Ben-

Hadad, which even now was ringed by Israeli ladders, the king drew the prophet close. "They say that Ashur-dan is holed up there with his Damascene allies." He winked. "Imagine, the armies of Jeroboam spitting in Assyria's face!" Then, throwing his head back, he clapped Jonah on the shoulder. "Perhaps the emperor will meet his final glory a little before his time!"

Jonah listened to his bravado appreciatively, a smile working at his lips. "Such a thing would be an unexpected blessing," he agreed.

"Tell me," Jeroboam spurred him, "do you have a prophecy concerning Ashur-dan? Will he survive the spears of Israel?"

But the seer said nothing, his attention drawn by the mourning of women in the Damascene streets, and by the closeted cries of children, too late hidden from the horrors of war.

Ashur-dan did survive the spears of Israel. While his allies succumbed to the invaders' blows, losing their territory to Palestine — many meeting death the night the citadel was stormed — the emperor escaped under cover of darkness, just before dawn.

While the Hebrews were diverted at the

center of town, his chariot fled unimpeded toward the desert gate. Jonah, standing with Jeroboam at the juncture of the eastern and southern walls, was the first to see him.

"Sir, could it be?" the son of Amittai marveled, clutching the king's arm and turning him toward the fleeing vehicle.

On the instant, Jeroboam left the watchtower and ordered men to pursue the Assyrian. But it was a tardy move. No Israeli would count Ashur-dan among his trophies that night. And no Hebrew would be able to touch him.

Only the prophet, left alone upon the wall, would challenge the emperor across the fields of war. And when he did it was without a weapon.

The King of the World, standing in his chariot, turned a fleeting glance toward the conquered city. But it was the simple seer who captured his eye, the lone figure in the tattered cloak, who had first spied him.

A peculiar uneasiness filled Ashur-dan at the sight of the solitary watcher — a spiritual dread, beyond the fear of war.

CHAPTER
9

Jonah had been with Jeroboam two years. With the prophet's encouragement and the alliance with Judah, the Hebrew territory had been expanded as Jonah had predicted, from Lebanon to the Dead Sea and from the Mediterranean through Trans-Jordan, reestablishing the original bounds of ancient Canaan.

Following the siege at Damascus, Jeroboam had boldly pursued the great city of Hamath, and, indeed, had overrun all of Syria, adding to the destruction that the barbarians of Ararat had already achieved along the northern reaches of that vast territory.

For Jeroboam, the rewards were more than political. They were personal as well. While he could glory in the fact that Hamath and Damascus were now his tributaries, paying him homage and revenue, his greatest fulfillment lay in the fact that he had brought to successful issue the wars that his father had undertaken. When he communed with the memory of his father, Joash, it was no longer in shame, but with head held high.

Currently, the lands of Judah and Israel approximated the same territory as that over which David and Solomon had ruled, and the two kingdoms enjoyed prosperity approaching that historic pinnacle.

Often these days, Jeroboam's dreams turned eastward, beyond Jordan, across the Arabian Desert, across the River Euphrates. Lust to crush the Dog of the Tigris began to dominate his thoughts, and while Jonah felt it his ministry to keep the king's eyes on God, he could not help but dream with him from time to time.

Though the prophet had frequently been accused by his fellow villagers of a too-liberal political bent, one which allowed him to accept Judeans as his brothers, he had no such altruistic tolerance for the Assyrians. He hated them with typical Palestinian zeal. Had he borne a spear at his side when he stood upon the Damascus wall, he likely would have thrust it toward Ashur-dan's fleeing chariot; and often he wished he had had more than the warning of Jehovah in his fist that night.

For the joys of success that God had bestowed on Israel were forever overshadowed by the fact that another power held the world in a stranglehold. As long as Assyria ruled, no subservient nation could realize its full potential.

Jonah knew that Jeroboam strained against this now, like a prisoner who had broken his own fetters only to become more aware of the stone walls that made up the dungeon. How long he would be content with the borders of David and Solomon, the prophet could not guess. But he sensed that the king was ready for greater things, even the challenging of Nineveh.

Jonah's spine tingled this evening as he walked down the broad corridor leading past the king's banquet hall. He had been invited to the festivities of a courtly dinner, one at which Jeroboam was to announce plans for the future. But he had declined, wishing to be alone.

Sounds of celebration and anticipation spilled from the dining room, but he tried to ignore them. He wished to spend time in prayer. Too rarely did the luxury of solitude present itself, and he pursued it quickly, exiting into a small courtyard that overlooked the road to Judah, past Beth-El.

Taking a deep breath of mountain air, he thought on the days of Amos, and remembered Amaziah, the high priest. He recalled the queen who had brought low the Israelite nation, and he pondered the unswerving vengeance of God.

But what of Amos himself? What had become of Jehovah's mighty spokesman? Strange, it seemed, that not only had the enemies of truth been eradicated, but the holy one who had heralded their demise had also vanished like a vapor.

Did he spend his days, now, plodding after sheep in the Judean hills? Did he long for public acclaim, or wonder why his star, which had burned so brightly, had been snuffed to silence?

Then Jonah considered himself, shuddering. Raised from poverty to feast beside princes, would he one day clean pots again and gather wool for the making of tents?

Suddenly fear seized him, and as he faced it, shame followed. What kinds of questions was he asking? Had he become so proud that the ways of his father, Amittai, were beneath him?

He knew better than to let such pride lodge long within his breast. "Forgive me," he whispered. "Let me be content to rise to glory with Jeroboam, or to comb goats' hair in Gath-hepher. Only crush the enemies of Israel, and give its people peace."

There was a work to be done in the prophet's heart, and it would begin that night.

When the preacher returned to his room, sleep would be brief. Barely had he placed his head upon his pillow, and barely had the webs of slumber begun to weave their tapestry, when a rumbling as of a mighty chariot roared through his head.

Sitting up with a jolt, he shook himself and turned over with a scowl.

But again, every time he came close to sleep, it was interrupted by the clatter of horses' hooves and the thunder of iron wheels.

Jonah swung his legs over the edge of the tall bed and peered fearfully about the vacant room. It must have been a dream that wakened him, and yet it had been so real, as though a careening cart speeded repeatedly across his very floor.

Walking to his chamber window, he sought to shake the peculiar nightmare by dwelling on the world outside. But now, fully awake, he heard the same storm of sound, and sensing it rush past him and across the palace walls, he was caught by a flash of gold upon the moonlit sands beyond.

"Could it be, sir?" he heard himself inquire, just as he had done that night on the Damascus wall. Surely he only imagined he saw Ashur-dan fleeing across the plain.

As though there were no space between them, the prophet could see the Assyrian's face. And its expression riveted his heart. For the emperor's eyes were pleading, and his hand was raised toward Jonah's window.

The prophet's skin crawled. Shielding himself, he cried out against the sight.

When he found courage to look again upon the plain, it was quiet. No chariot was visible, no roar of iron wheels could be discerned. Though only seconds had passed, there was no trace of the Ninevite, and Jonah passed the night in sleepless wonder.

CHAPTER
10

The fact that an Assyrian emperor would go out of his way to be present at the siege of Damascus testified to the strategic and financial importance of Syria.

As the land bridge between Asia and Africa, she was the natural route for armies traveling east, west, north, or south, and arteries of trade from any nation converged on her principal cities.

For wealth, Syria could not be equaled. Her cedar and cypress forests, famed for their oils and resins, were coveted by every land. For figs, olives, plums, pears, apples, and dates, she had no rival, and her wines were purchased by every country in the world. Foreigners looked to her for papyrus, and for the products of her medicinal and aromatic plants. For cattle, for minerals, vegetables, terebinth, sumac and laurel wood, cinnabar, alabaster, amber and gypsum, she was a treasure.

Therefore it was no small thing when she fell to Israel from her southern borders, while her northern edge belonged to the barbaric invaders.

Such a loss produced a gaping hole in the imperial map, not only geographically, but militarily and materially.

It was little wonder that Ashur-dan trembled. It was not beyond belief that Israel might turn on Nineveh itself, for she now held one of the most important blocs in the Fertile Crescent. And it was no wonder that the emperor was forced to consider Jeroboam his most feared rival, though previously he had merited not the least interest on the part of Nineveh.

Ashur-dan could look east to Iran for iron and horses, the materiel of war machines. In this he took some comfort. But Israeli ownership of Syria impeded traffic with his Egyptian satellites, the Mediterranean coast — and, with the influence of the Ararat mountaineers, even the commercial colonies of Anatolia and Cappadocia to the north.

Using political diplomacy, he was just beginning to win the alliance of Iran against any eventual Israeli invasion when calamity of another sort struck the capital.

It began with a portentous reading of the

144

stars by the wisemen of his court. "Plague," they told him, "striking the nobility first and then spreading throughout Nineveh and its suburbs."

"When?" the emperor inquired, not daring to doubt the predictions of the astrologers who had served the palace admirably for generations.

Consulting together, they approached him after many days, and huddling upon the stateroom carpet, presented a puzzling reply. "Our readings tell us, O Majesty, a peculiar thing. 'Before the emperor repents,' the constellations say, 'the ailment of the air shall descend.'"

Ashur-dan, leaning down from his throne, scrutinized the sages narrowly. "Before I repent! What foolishness is this?"

"We have no interpretation, sir," the eldest answered. "We only know what the stars say."

The emperor, dissatisfied, grew angry and railed, "Am I not loyal to all the gods? What monarch has paid more revenue to Asshur than I? Who has kept up the houses of Ishtar and Ramman, or any of the triads more perfectly than I?"

The magi leaned together, shrugging and shaking their heads, but Ashur-dan had no patience. "Find me a god to whom

I have not paid due respect! Go ahead! Seek!" he cried, thrusting them from the room. "From Egypt to Babylon, I honor the deities of my people!"

The wisemen could not deny their master's religious zeal. They could not readily name any deity whom he might have overlooked in the division of funds or the appointment of holidays.

Red-faced, they left his presence, not knowing whether to take his command to heart or not. But just in case he did desire an accounting, they would research for him. They would summon reports from the temples of every god in the empire, and they would tabulate a record of Ashurdan's benevolences. Perhaps the offended stars could be deterred from their judgment, convinced that they were mistaken after all.

Jonah knew little of stars and suns. The reading of orbits and of moons was not only foreign to him, but pagan. If there were truth to be found in such things, it was subservient to the truth of Jehovah, and the oracles to which his people alone were privy.

But he was receiving his own messages, and had he known that they corresponded with the fearsome signs chronicled by Assyrian sages, he might have feared even more for his own mind.

He had not yet told Jeroboam about his strange visions, the repeated sightings of Ashur-dan pleading for his help. They came in various forms, from the gesture in the fleeing chariot to more pointed petitions: the emperor waking him from sound sleep night after night, standing beside his bed with outstretched hands.

The omens repelled the prophet. Surely they were the devil's doings, he reasoned. The work of Jehovah did not involve Gentiles, except as they were used by God to chasten his people.

Still, though he begged for the visions to cease, and for his focus on Israel to be renewed, the specter of Ashur-dan grew more persistent, the ominous pleadings more frequent.

When word swept across the empire that a rash of nameless diseases had ravaged the palace at Nineveh, Jonah was strangely troubled, experiencing an anxiety for the capital that was out of place in the heart of a Hebrew.

Indeed, compassion for Assyria had crept into his soul, and he did not like the feeling.

CHAPTER
11

Ashur-dan's younger sister could have passed for barely more than a child. Fragile and petite, she wore her aristocracy with feminine grace, and with a humility rarely seen among royalty.

The emperor loved her more than he loved any other human being. In fact, he loved no one else. She had been his charge since she was tiny, their mother and father having been too distracted by the pleasures of courtly life and the pursuit of glory. She filled the void he had allowed no one else to occupy, for a sense of family and for tenderness.

Today he sat at her bedside, as he had done almost without a break for three days and nights. The plague prophesied by the palace seers had first struck the nobility, as predicted, and was spreading now throughout the capital and its suburbs. Kisha, the porcelain-cheeked damsel, the sole focus of caring in his life, lay in restless fever upon her bed. She had been one of the first to succumb to the infection.

Only in delirium had her eyes fluttered open since she had fallen into a flushed slumber thirty-six hours before. Ashur-dan held her limp hand, his head resting upon her bed, as he dozed intermittently. His physicians had warned him not to hover so close, lest he contract the disease and the empire be left to chaos. But he would not heed their advice.

Just now he roused, and as always, his eyes traveled instantly to the maiden's face. "Has she moved?" he asked.

The matron commissioned to keep records of her condition shook her head sadly. "There is no change, sir," she replied.

Ashur-dan stood up and sighed. Drawing Kisha's hot hand to his lips, he brushed it with a kiss, then turned for the door.

His voice was low and foreboding as he walked into the hall and ordered his guards to call for the astrologers. When the stargazers arrived, it was with trepidation.

"But, sir, we have given you our reports," they protested, gathering again in his stateroom. "Every shrine, every holy place, and every temple from the Tigris to the Nile has been sending an account of your contributions and benevolences. Not one has been dissatisfied. All praise your equanimity."

The emperor glared at the magicians, curbing the desire to avenge himself on them. "By all the gods, then," he cried, "what foolishness did you hand me weeks ago? If I have not offended any deity, for what am I to repent?"

Again the prophets were bewildered, and when they could only look at one another sheepishly, the monarch lost all patience.

His face clouding, he thundered, "My sister lies dying, and all you can tell me is that some unknown sin on my part has brought this plague upon my house and upon our people! Worthless wisemen are you all!" he shouted, driving them from his presence.

"Perhaps, Your Majesty," the eldest faltered as he exited the emperor's chamber, "perhaps there will yet be light shed on this matter. There are a few replies outstanding."

"From which temples?" he bellowed. "What priest of what god would be so foolish as to delay response?"

The seer trembled, his companions standing close at his back, fearing to look the ruler in the eye.

"Actually, sir, there are only two. . . ."

"Yes?"

The star-seeker shuffled his feet and cleared his throat. "Your enemies, sir . . . Uzziah and Jeroboam."

"Speak up! Whom did you name?"

"Judah and Israel, sir, have not replied. Your enemies, Uzziah and Jeroboam of Judah and . . . Israel."

Ashur-dan's face grew pale, and his focus riveted on the old sage.

But somehow it made sense, what he was hearing. Of course! The rise of Israel had always seemed a more-than-human success, almost as though some supernatural force were behind it.

Ashur-dan's mind flashed from the fall of Damascus to the peculiar fellow whom he had seen standing upon its wall the night he fled the city. Except for his shabby cloak, there had been nothing noteworthy in his appearance. But the stranger had impressed the emperor with more than physical presence. Something in his ominous gaze had left its mark upon Ashur-dan's soul.

CHAPTER
12

Jonah was summoned to Jeroboam's chamber after another night of interrupted sleep. He tried, through an exhausted haze, to show due interest in the king's enthusiastic plans.

He was sharing his intention to push east of Damascus, toward Haran first and then . . . Nineveh. Of course, he was hoping for Jonah's blessing on his scheme, since the tentmaker's son had been his spiritual advisor through all his successful ventures.

The consultant showed no reluctance to endorse his ambitions. But whenever the names of Nineveh or Ashur-dan were spoken, weariness swept fresh over the prophet, and, try as he might, he could not give Jeroboam his full attention.

When the king at last asked his opinion on the proposed strategies, he contemplated the issue through a bleary fog.

"Jonah!" Jeroboam laughed. "What is it?

I feel you are wandering far beyond the walls of this room." Drawing near, he surveyed the preacher closely. "You do not look well of late, my friend. Are you ill?" he inquired.

The counselor knew that the last few times he had been in the king's presence, he had been a less than sparkling companion.

"I am well, sir," he replied. "Perhaps just a bit . . . homesick," he hedged. "I have not seen my father in years."

Jeroboam's eyes brightened. "Why — of course!" he agreed. "I am sorry I did not guess as much. You have been away from those you love far too long."

Jonah relaxed and smiled a little. His explanation had, after all, not been complete falsehood. He thought on his father and the quiet village of his childhood very often these days, wishing for Amittai's simple wisdom and guiding counsel.

"Well," Jeroboam said, clapping him on the back, "if I have your approval of my plans, I can proceed without you. I want you to take a short respite in Gath-hepher. Go visit your family and friends. We will all benefit from your gaining a much-deserved rest."

The young man had not expected such a

reprieve, nor would he ever have asked it of his own accord. "Perhaps a change would do me good," he said, sighing more heavily than he intended.

The king studied him with concern, then led him to the door. "Indeed." He nodded. "And when you return, I know God will use you for Israel's sake . . . more mightily than ever."

By evening, Jonah was well on the way to Gath-hepher. But he had gotten a late start, and would be obliged to sleep one night on the road.

The king had offered him a royal chauffeur, a chariot of his own to carry him home, and a personal valet. But he had refused the luxuries, preferring to be alone. When night fell, he was especially glad for that decision.

There was, to be sure, the ever-present fear of bandits along the way, and of wild beasts prowling the empty outback. But the tormented seer could not predict what peculiar journeys of spirit might be his during slumber, or what phantoms might interrupt his sleep. He wished for no one to witness his dialogues with the intangible, and chose to take his chances on his own.

The spot along the road where he would

bed down for the night was a caravan stop-off. Jonah picked a place beneath a palm tree, some distance from a noisy group of camel traders. He sought a measure of peace by burying his head in his rolled-up cloak. He had left the mantle of Amos behind, as it was a holy garment, not intended for mundane activities. And, besides, he never would have used it as a pillow.

Somehow he was able to fall asleep amid his neighbors' fighting and rowdy laughter, even though the balm of slumber had eluded him in the quiet palace, nights on end.

But the blessed reprieve was short-lived. At some point after even the lusty campers had begun to settle down, he felt someone tap his shoulder, and he opened his heavy eyelids with much difficulty.

Assuming it must be some fellow traveler, he leaned upon one elbow and looked for the source of the sensation.

No one was nearby, and instantly his skin crawled. "Lord, no," he whispered. "Not here. Not now. . . ."

But it was to be as he feared. The touch was followed by a voice — which none but Jonah heard.

In the past, the phenomenon had been

accompanied by a vision of Ashur-dan, who did the speaking. Tonight, there was no phantom emperor. No vision whatever came with the message, and the call was of a different sort: an inner prompting, as of the voice of . . . God.

"Arise! Go to Nineveh the Great City and cry against it! For their wickedness has come up before me," it declared.

Jonah, sitting upright, drew his knees beneath his chin, and shivered. "Who are you, Lord?" he asked aloud.

When he placed his fists to his ears, the caravaneers, noting his peculiar behavior, peered at one another warily.

Still he continued what seemed to be a one-sided conversation, staring into the air and shaking his head.

"No!" he cried. "Surely this is not your will, my God! If I preach in Nineveh, they may, perchance, repent. And if they repent, I know you! You are a gracious and compassionate God, slow to anger, abundant in loving-kindness, and one who relents concerning calamity! I know that you would turn back the armies of Jeroboam and withdraw your judgment from the cursed Assyrians!"

Now the camel drivers rolled their eyes and, watching the peculiar ravings of the lone stranger, began to mock him. One pantomimed Jonah's supposed imbibing, suggesting that he must be drunk. Another held his own head and staggered like a lunatic about the camp.

They could make no sense of his importunate wailing, as Jonah rocked to and fro upon his haunches, pleading with the Almighty against some dreadful directive.

Tears and spittle mingled in the prophet's beard, as he, crazed with weariness and fear, fought Jehovah's inscrutable challenge. When he rose from his pallet of dirt, stumbling solitary into the wilderness night, they laughed the louder, and did not ask where he was going.

CHAPTER
13

Jonah went no further toward home than the oasis where he had encountered God's voice. In fact, when he stumbled out into the dark, it was in the opposite direction.

When dawn arrived, he found himself heading west, away from Gath-hepher, and certainly away from any road leading to Nineveh.

The oasis had been at the junction of two main highways, one leading back toward Samaria, the other along the Plain of Sharon toward the coast.

Jonah had not intended to pick this route. When he had run from Jehovah's voice and from the tauntings of his fellow humans, he had not selected any particular destination. He could just as easily have returned to the familiarity of the palace. But when he realized, with the brightening of day and the appearance of merchant trains along his path, that he was headed for the Great Sea, he found himself taking a perverse relief in the prospect.

Jonah had been brought up in the ways of God. Had he not been a prophet, a preacher in Israel? He knew better, intellectually and spiritually, than to think any man capable of escaping the Almighty.

But the mind is a crooked thing, and the soul that hides itself is the most exposed of all to guilt and anxiety. With each step the fugitive took away from his appointed mission, the heavier did those emotions weigh upon him.

Nevertheless, he did continue to put one foot in front of the other toward the Mediterranean. He continued to flee the hounding call of God: "Go to Nineveh and cry against it! *Cry against it!*"

When the air south of Mt. Carmel and west of Shechem began to smell of oak forests and salt breezes, his heart raced with his feet, nudging him faster.

The coast of Palestine was devoid of natural harbors. Save for the spot at which Carmel protruded into the Great Sea, it was perfectly straight. Therefore, the Israelites were inland, mountain people, not maritime folk. But the Plain of Sharon was the one parcel of coastland under their control; and the harbor at Joppa, while not comparable to Phoenicia's fine ports at Tyre and Sidon, was a useful site for Jerusalem's African and European trade.

Were Jonah to follow the road he was on until it reached the small town of Lod, then turn due west, he could reach Joppa before nightfall. He feared to speculate beyond that point.

Studying the dusty thoroughfare, he glimpsed his flashing sandals, and realized that he was running. He slowed his pace to a walk, an embarrassed flush rising to his cheeks. His pulse pounded in his ears, and he wondered how long he had been keeping up such a rapid gait.

Most of the time he was not even cognizant of his own body, or of the peculiar sight he must have made, sweat-streaked, hunched, and bedraggled, fleeing down the busy highway. Occasionally he was aware of the pedestrians, riders, and drivers who searched the road behind him, trying to spy his invisible pursuer. But he had no pride to stop himself, and too much fear to reconsider his position.

Twice as a child he had accompanied his father to Joppa, when the tentmaker arranged a rare export of his products. The ruddy hues of its sifting dunes and the glory of its dense oak hills remained a vivid memory. Today, when the fertile Sharon plain began to reveal red sand mixed with the earth, he knew he was nearing the sea.

Granules of the scarlet grit worked their way between his toes and clung to the perspiring skin beneath his sandal straps. He was close to the port city when he stopped along the road to loosen his shoes and beat out the irritating accumulation.

Resting upon a wayside bench, he joined with other travelers coming or going, most accompanied by wagons and heavily laden beasts. He did not realize how out of place he appeared, until a kind-faced woman approached him.

She was very old, apparently the wife of an equally aged merchant with whom she traveled; she had likely journeyed this route countless times. Leaning over Jonah, who was himself bent over, cleaning his sandals, she whispered, "Is there anything we can do?"

Jonah lurched into the moment and stared up at her, his eyes wild. "What?"

"I say, is there anything we can do?" she repeated. "My husband and I try to help troubled folk whenever we can."

The fugitive glanced in the direction of her gesture, and seeing the merchant's concerned expression, turned his head in shame. Suddenly, he sensed his criminal condition, and began to feel the impact of his disobedience. He quickly surveyed his dusty cloak and tear-stained tunic, chagrined at her offer.

"Madam," he said in a strangled tone, "you obviously do not know who I am."

The words "Jeroboam" and "palace," "prophet" and "preacher," tumbled out in a rush of self-defense. The woman studied him, wide eyed. Quickly, however, her husband approached and, whispering something in her ear, drew her away.

Her face was pale as she mounted the seat beside the merchant; and as he hastened his small train down the highway, she peered fearfully over her shoulder, her spouse muttering beneath his breath and shaking his head.

"We must be more careful upon the road these days," he was objecting. "Too many peculiar folk about."

Jonah would have taken offense, but he feared more for his own mind than he cared about their disdain. Leaning down, he grasped his sandals and secured them hastily to his feet.

If only he could quiet his racing thoughts. If only . . .

But the red of sunset was mingling now with Sharon's rusty slopes. If he hoped to reach Joppa before dark, he must be moving on.

CHAPTER
14

Though Jonah did not admit it to himself, his intention, once he reached Joppa, was to book passage on any ship heading west — and the farther west the better.

Visions of Gibraltar and the straits at the far end of the Great Sea came often to mind as he fled down the highway. Even the name of the famous Spanish refinery town, Tarshish, tempted him over and over.

It was not peculiar that he should single out such specific sites in his fantasy of escape. Though he had never traveled beyond the boundaries of Palestine, the names of Gibraltar and Spain represented the ends of the earth. They spoke of escape from all that was familiar and confining; of adventure and anonymity — the latter being of particular value to one who ran from God.

Therefore, though Jonah had not borne

in mind any particular destination when he fled the camel herders, the closer he came to the sea, the more the dream of foreign shores lured him.

For the Hebrew ran not only from Jehovah, but from Jeroboam, from Israel, and from his upbringing. He was of all men to be pitied; for in choosing to avoid his calling, he risked becoming a vagabond, a man without a country or a faith.

There had always been nomads on the earth — folk who made their living free from political loyalties and national ties. There were self-made itinerants who simply preferred to live on the road, surviving hand to mouth. Such people were not pitied; they were, in fact, often envied and admired for their freedom.

But Jonah was not of either sort. He had stood before princes and had been counselor to a king. He had lived in luxury and known the respect of an entire land. Jonah had been a prophet of God.

As he walked the empty docks of Joppa, enduring another guilt-ridden and sleepless night, he watched the blue-white sheen off the Mediterranean moon as it played with the rippling sea. Solomon had used these very waters to transport timber for his temple, lashing it together in immense, raftlike barges, and floating it down from Lebanon. But more typically, Israel bowed the maritime knee to Phoenicia and to distant colonies of Africa and Europe, and no Hebrew was much at home in a seaport.

Tonight, the silvery orb, the same one that Marna and Jeroboam had courted from their private balcony, was fuller and larger than the preacher had ever seen it. Something about his proximity to the western waters made it seem much closer, almost as though he could reach out and touch it.

He thought of the harlot-queen who had been exiled back to the coast; and remembering that Amaziah had joined her there, Jonah felt his own alien condition even more strongly. While Marna and the priest had been God's enemies, the tentmaker's son had worked for their displacement. Yet now, he, just as surely, was in exile.

The fugitive sat down upon a piling near the lapping waters and drew his knees up under his chin. Closing his eyes, he tried to shut out such comparisons. Surely, he still argued, the hounding voice that insisted he go to Assyria was not of the Lord. He must be overtaxed. Time away from all that was familiar would do him good. Hadn't Jeroboam said he needed rest?

And what would his own father, Amittai, say — the political thinker who could not even accept Judeans as his brethren? Would he not agree that such a proposition as a mission to Assyria was devilish?

Of course, Jonah assured himself. Neither king nor country, brotherhood nor family, would endorse such a notion. A vacation would clear his head of the foolishness.

Still, as he waited through the lonely night, he longed for the sounds of commerce and industry that morning would bring. Human life in all its thoughtless activity would relieve him of morbid introspection.

Something, indeed, *must* relieve him, or he would go mad.

When dawn spilled over Joppa, it seemed the whole world blazed white. "Beauty," the town's name implied — and deservedly so.

The city's pristine walls, and her terraced hills, layered with pale stone houses, reflected such a mass of sunshine, it seemed the place was newborn each morning and not its nearly eight centuries old.

Assigned to the tribe of Dan, it had not come under Israelite control until David had taken the coast. Cradled between the slopes of the central range and the sycamore forests of the southern Shephelah, it had been the contested envy of more than one conqueror.

When Jonah was awakened by the massaging sun and by sounds of traffic on the wharves, he sat erect and rubbed the blare of light from his offended eyes. Blinking, he stood and surveyed the scene before him: the nearly frenzied movement of sailors and cargo-haulers as they went about their tasks, loading and unloading vessels, arranging for their masters' day at market and shouting instructions over the din of wheels and clatter of hooves.

All business led inevitably toward the massive gates of the city; and as Jonah watched the gigantic doors of Joppa open for the flow of trade, he remembered the popular tale of an Egyptian general who had lived seven hundred years before. Feigning surrender after an attempt to take the seaport, he had ordered two hundred of his soldiers to climb into large baskets, and five hundred to carry them. Pretending that the containers were filled with booty that the "vanquished" invaders were offering to their conquerors, he commanded his men to march toward the gates.

The pleased king of Joppa had opened the great doors to receive the bounty; but once inside, the smuggled Egyptians overwhelmed their surprised hosts, claiming the town in the name of Pharaoh.

Likely this very day there were, among the numerous nationalities represented, many sea lords who coveted the wealth of Joppa. Jonah could distinguish ships of the Egyptians, Mesopotamians, and Babylonians in the tidy port, their large, striped sails emblazoned with symbols of gods and kings.

The variety of vessels was a veritable stockyard of seaworthy transportation. It took little familiarity with things nautical to determine their uses. Here was a giant barge for the hauling of heavy cargo over long distances. There was a passenger boat with wide decks and ornate, many-windowed terraces. Commercial barks were very practical, their deep bodies the storehouse of treasures, and their only adornment the carved prows which rose up in sensuous likenesses of Astarte or Ishtar.

The black-shrouded raft across the way had to be a funeral float, and the numerous oaken oars that jutted from the portholes of many a ship bespoke the slave labor employed to propel them. But, for the most part, the harbor was a lively place, its multicolored sails and cedar masts, lavish ornamentation of ivory and inlaid boxwood, filling the eye with crafted wonder.

All this Jonah could appreciate, even in his preoccupied state. But he did not linger over these sights. Scanning the docks, he sought vessels equipped for the longest journeys. And steeling himself against God's pursuing tread, he set his mind for faraway places.

CHAPTER
15

Some of the merchant ships fastened in Joppa's harbor were small vessels, having no hold, their cargo stored on deck in heavy burlap wrappers or wooden crates. These boats Jonah passed by, though they by far outnumbered the larger sort.

What he aimed for were the spacious ships with the fat bellies, their treasures hidden in cradlelike sanctuaries, nestled deep in the water. Such vessels, hc knew, would be plying the sea away from Palestine, far to the west.

At last he spied a glorious craft, a bireme, equipped with two banks of oars and, hence, many galley slaves. It must be a speedy vessel, he reasoned, with so much power behind its prow. Its stem and stern were similar in shape, except that the bow swept forward and up, arrowlike, and was adorned with a gigantic carving of a waterfowl, its chest protruding and its head stretched across the water.

As he rushed down the dock, he could see, through its open railing, that the boat's tackling included not only a large mast and yard arm, but several other masts of smaller dimension, and a foresail for stormy weather. Though the multicolored sheets were presently rolled up and lashed to the rigging, they appeared to be of the finest byssus linen, a fabric which his father had always coveted for his most expensive projects.

Even the stern sported an ample awning of the same material, in a rainbow of stripes and insignias. Jonah's eyes quickly traveled to the prow, where the likeness of colossal fish eyes ornamented the sides of the ship, giving it an almost animated effect as it bobbed lazily beside the dock. Above the eyes were the same insignias that the awning bore, apparently the crests and badges of the owner's family and town.

Though Jonah was not well versed in heraldry, he assumed the emblems were of Phoenician origin, for they contained letters of that famed alphabet, the envy of the literate world for simplicity and convenience.

"Likely a Tyrian or Sidonian," Jonah

muttered, not at all eager to commit his well-being to a pagan host. But he would have little choice, the great majority of the harbor's patrons being from outside Israel.

Nor would he have to speculate for long, as a figure of some importance had just mounted the deck and taken a seat beneath the awning. Placing a papyrus scroll on a small table before him, the man unrolled it and began to write.

Jonah, suddenly reminded of his disheveled appearance, smoothed his hair and straightened his cloak. Stuffing his satchel beneath his arm, he took a deep breath and stepped toward the pier. Within the satchel was only an extra pair of sandals and another light cloak, all he had thought he could possibly need between the palace and Gath-hepher. The single loaf of bread he had carried had long since been eaten on the run, and he hoped, now, that he had brought enough money to afford passage.

How could he have been so foolish as to come this far without thought to expenses? Was he indeed losing his mind?

Halting midway between the harbor road and the dock, he reached for the small purse which hung upon his girdle, and opened it with trembling fingers. But just as he was about to dump the contents into his palm, relief swept over him. *Yes,* surely it was still there — the gold piece that Jeroboam had slipped to him as he had left the palace. "Give this to your father," the king had insisted, "for your maintenance. You are, after all, a member of *my* house now."

Ah — there it was! In the very bottom of the pouch. Jonah drew it out and cradled it in his sweaty hand, turning it over and over in the sun. The king had, of course, meant it as a gift to Amittai, rather than as repayment for any expenses he would incur as Jonah's host. A token from the palace of Jeroboam would, indeed, have paid for a month's lodging at the finest inn in Israel.

The fact that the prophet was adding robbery to his criminal record troubled him little. What did trouble him, as he buried the coin again, was the tramping sound which had filled his ears and buzzed inside his head since dawn — the sound as of an army chasing him.

The hosts of heaven, his conscience warned, *the tenacious, hounding hosts of God.*

It was from this that he fled as he stepped onto the gently swaying dock and walked toward the waiting ship. It was from the knowledge of his own wrongdoing that he sought escape.

The vessel's owner was unaware of his

struggle as he approached the awning, and was even unaware of Jonah, himself, until the Hebrew cleared his throat several times. Looking up with a start, the ship's master glared angrily at the interruption.

"We can take no passengers this voyage!" he asserted. "Our hold is full of cargo."

Jonah knew he spoke the truth, for the papyrus upon which he calculated his inventory was laden with figures. As the man surveyed his unkempt clothes and ragged beard, he became even more adamant. "Go away, fellow!" he urged. "You'll find no passage here!"

"But, sir, I would pay dearly for your help," the vagabond pleaded. "It is most urgent that I leave . . . that I go west."

At this, he fumbled through his pouch, searching for the heavy coin. But the master only shook his head and stood up from the table.

Near the ship's helm, the second officer, pilot or captain of the vessel, was conferring with the steersman. Distracted by the owner's strange behavior, both men came quickly to his assistance.

"Is this man troubling you, master?" the pilot inquired.

The owner leaned toward him in a quick exchange, as Jonah rifled the purse. The would-be passenger caught only a few syllables — "vagrant" at best and "fugitive" at worst — enough to know that he was suspect on more than one level.

But just as the steersman moved to evict him, Jonah produced the gold piece, and the Phoenicians turned pale.

Grasping the coin from the Hebrew's hand, the pilot passed it to the master, who studied it with amazement. "The seal of Jeroboam!" he marveled, noting the insignia. "You would be from Samaria?"

"I am," Jonah replied.

Now the seamen were even more suspicious of the newcomer. Only servants of a nation's palace carried tokens bearing a monarch's seal. But when the steersman opened his mouth to question the stranger, the master hushed him quickly.

Not about to lose a royal gold piece for the sake of scrupulosity, he suddenly changed his tone. His face, once full of objection, now bore a solicitous smile.

"Pardon our hesitation," he apologized, taking Jonah by the arm and leading him toward the stairs down to the passenger compartment. "I only fear that our accommodations are not worthy of your station."

The guest nodded patiently as the host showed him to the chamber, not in the least impressed by the merchant's fawning.

What did impress him was the sight of the plump hammock strung between two posts of the cozy but ornate room. As the master bowed graciously out the door, closing it behind him and still muttering apologies, Jonah climbed into the swinging bed and buried his head in the downy pillow. Once he began to doze, the tramping sounds of Jehovah's pursuit grew dim.

He had forgotten to ask the captain's destination, but any spot on earth, seaward from Nineveh, was satisfactory.

PART THREE

HELL

Lest . . . when I have preached to others, I myself should be a castaway.

1 CORINTHIANS 9:27

CHAPTER
1

Kisha, the Assyrian princess, fidgeted with the neckline of her silk tunic and turned restlessly upon her bed. The matron who had sat watch beside her for the past two days studied the young woman in surprise.

It appeared that she was rousing from her week-long sleep, and that at any moment she might open her eyes.

When the dark-fringed lids did flutter, and when the girl peered dazedly about the room, the matron rushed for the door.

"Call the emperor!" she commanded.

Within minutes Ashur-dan stood at Kisha's pillow. Taking her frail hand, he kissed it lightly and breathed over her with soft whispers. "Sister," he pleaded, "return to us. . . ."

The fragile maiden opened her eyes again, and seemed to recognize her brother. "Dan?" she replied, using the nickname only she was privileged to utter.

The emperor started, tears trembling along his lashes. "Yes," he declared, trying to contain his joy. "I am here!"

"There is weeping in the streets," the princess whimpered. "Weeping in Nineveh."

The monarch glanced at the matron, who only shrugged; then he studied the fevered countenance once again. "Rest now," he said, his tone soothing, despite the grisly reminder.

But Kisha was insistent, tossing upon her pillow as though she were at war. "Through my sickness I wandered the streets." She sighed. "Our people die. Children die."

She ran her limp fingers down the royal blue of Ashur-dan's garment and fumbled with the gold fringe that draped his torso from shoulder to waist. Grasping him to her, she groaned, "Where is your crown, my lord? Perhaps your crown can ward off the evil. . . ."

As she then caressed his crimped beard and the tight braids which rested upon the nape of his neck, he studied her warily. "Little one," he responded, "I wear a crown only when I go before my ministers or my people. But see here," he directed, lifting her hand to his forehead, "a gold wreath upon my brow. . . ."

Kisha lay back against her pillow, her dark tresses contrasting starkly with the linen and with the white of her pallid skin. "No, my lord," she objected, "you are royalty. Surely, if you wear your crown, the evil will depart."

Her words began to ramble nonsensically, and Ashur-dan placed her hand again upon her breast. Never had he felt the weight of imperial responsibility so keenly as he did at this moment. And never had he felt so impotent.

"Tell me if there is further improvement," he instructed the matron. And with stooped shoulders he left the chamber.

A breeze off the Tigris played with the broad leaves of Ashur-dan's grape arbor and wove itself around the blue-purple clusters, wafting their pungent aroma over the arboretum.

The emperor had purposely surrounded himself with people this afternoon, calling for all his musicians, his personal servants, and his fanbearers to accompany him on a tour of the palace gardens. Long, sleek hounds basked in the shade of his elevated couch, as he rested now in the palm grove, speaking of trivial things with his ministers.

He reached down a regal toe to stroke the neck of his favorite mastiff, and tossed it a crumb from the sweet cake atop his red-enameled table. Sound and color were his companions today. "Wear your most festive garb," he had told his counselors. He himself had selected an emerald tunic — one with silver piping and a ruby-jeweled bodice. Plump pink pomegranates, soft brown rolls laced with golden honey, and small green onions complemented his clear white wine. And all talk was calculated to be frivolous.

With the rhythm of hip-slung drums and shoulder-borne harps, his musicians provoked the sinewy thighs and bare arms of dancing girls to sway and gyrate. One could have easily thought the times of Shalmaneser had returned to the palace grounds.

It was not a party, for Ashur-dan was not one for parties. But it was as close to a royal fling as the court had seen since the days of his father.

The emperor's smile was a little forced, however. And his idle chit-chat a bit unnatural. For not only was he unused to such things, but he fought the heaviness of recent days with belated urgency.

His ministers, too, were awkward with their new role. They had never before been required to entertain His Majesty. Their object, in his scheme, had always been to advise him in matters of conquest, acquisition, and expansion. But they were bound to please him, so today they kept their conversation airy.

Notable for their absence were the court magicians, those stargazers who had first brought word of the plague. Ashur-dan had made sure they were deleted from the day's company, as he sought to free himself, however temporarily, from their foreboding prognoses.

He drew a gilded coverlet over his feet and watched the amply endowed dancers with strained zeal. The wine had begun to loosen the tension in his neck and shoulders, however, when a small boy appeared at the garden gate.

Recognizing him as one of the palace's distance-running messengers, hired for fleetness of foot and extraordinary stamina, the king sat up uneasily. One of the servants, stationed at the gate to keep out intruders, struggled with the lad, who seemed most insistent on delivering a parchment.

Ashur-dan, sensing more bad news, nonetheless motioned to the gatekeeper to admit the boy.

The messenger raced to the emperor's couch, and falling before him, held the parchment aloft. "I was just returning from an errand to Haran, when I encountered a runner from Israel, O King," he panted. "He bade me take this directly to you, saying it was long-awaited word from your servant, Jeroboam."

The emperor's heart stuttered as he opened the waxen seal. And as he read the contents, his face grew as pale as any plague-stricken Ninevite's.

"To my lord, Ashur-dan, King of the World," it stated, "from your servant, Jeroboam, King of the Chosen Race: In reply to your decree for an accounting, let it be known that your benevolences to our temples and our faith, though forever generous and timely, are of no avail in the eyes of Jehovah, the One True God. And let it be known that, since you did not deign to lift a hand when we suffered under disease and famine, we will not stoop to lift you from the dust when El Shaddai crushes you with his foot. For the time is coming, O Emperor, and already is, when they shall say, 'Where is Nineveh the Great? And who is Ashur-dan?'

"For your cruelties and the cruelties of your fathers will come to an end — the evil with which you have oppressed all peoples, from the Tigris to the land beyond the Nile, from Taurus to the desert of Arabah.

"The time is coming and already is, O King."

CHAPTER
2

Jonah was asleep in the hold of the ship when it pulled out from the Joppa port. He was not privileged to see the armada of seagoing vessels that left the harbor at the same time — the large Egyptian galleys with their sharply upturned prows and gondolalike bodies, or the round, basketlike barks of Mesopotamia, whose components had been carted to the Great Sea from the inland desert and then constructed in this part of the world. He did not watch the entrance of Assyrian craft — skin and timber rafts supported on inflated hides, which normally sailed the Persian Gulf and the Gulf of Suez. Nor did he witness the comings and goings of the wealthy descendants of Minoan and Cretan sea kings, who sailed from Knossos to Troy, Athens, Asia Minor, and Ugarit in northern Syria, or from Phaestos to northern Africa and Egypt.

Compared to these great craft, the Phoenician ship could have been mistaken for a good-sized fishing boat; but it, like all its sisters, was so skillfully made and professionally manned, it took its place among the most powerful.

Jonah missed all this, but he did enjoy a deep, dreamless sleep — one in which no emperor intruded and no deity imposed his will.

When the tentmaker's son did finally rouse, the ship had been at sea over two days. It hugged the northern coast of Egypt, aiming for Tanis, when Jonah stumbled forth from the cradling hammock and opened his chamber door upon the dark storage compartment that sprawled beneath the main deck.

It took him some moments to realize where he was and what he was doing here. The humid cold of the deep-bellied hull sent a chill to his heart. As his eyes slowly adjusted to the faint dawn light spilling through floor timbers above, the large bundles and sacks of cargo stored all about appeared ghostly and still, like silent, scrutinizing passengers.

As reality seeped into his consciousness, he pieced the memory of past days into a credible whole. Yes — he was running from God Almighty — or from some impersonating spirit, some imposter demon who would have him go to . . . Nineveh. He was heading west aboard a pagan vessel, having left all he had ever known to seek escape.

The aromas of the hold told him this ship was a "Byblos traveler," a bearer of papyrus pith to some alien shore that had no resource for the making of scrolls and paper. With the odor of compressed reed strips and mulled thicket grass, there mingled other fragrances: the perfume of Syrian wine, Gilead oils, and Lebanon lumber.

And the vessel undoubtedly carried the purple dyes and glasswork for which the Phoenicians were famous. But as his vision became clearer, Jonah spied a row of mummy cases lining the far wall, and his skin bristled in obstinate bumps. The dreaming faces of Egyptians yet to be buried seemed to leer at him through closed eyes, lifelike visages painted upon the empty cases. And with the rocking of the ship, they swayed a little, appearing to lean together in analytic whispers.

"Who is he?" they seemed to ask. "And what is his crime?"

Jonah fumbled for the stairs, and, trying to shake the illusion, scrambled up the ladder and reached for the trapdoor in the ceiling. Giving little thought to his appearance, he bolted onto the deck, falling to his knees in his haste, and sprawling disgracefully upon the floor.

Raising his face, he found that two sandaled feet, heavily bound with stockings against the briny cold, stood alongside his nose. As he lifted his gaze up the length of someone's fine woolen robe, he trembled with chagrin. Indeed, it was the master of the trading vessel, the wealthy merchant who had first denied him passage.

Jonah could see from the man's disgusted expression that he wondered again if his decision to admit the Hebrew had been a wise one.

The disheveled passenger gathered his tunic tightly against his chest and tried to wipe the confusion from his face. "I . . . I dreamed a strange dream," he explained, rising to his knees. "Mummies were chasing me. . . ."

But even as he spoke, he knew how insane his own words sounded.

All about the deck, other men had gathered, peering at him in curiosity. Quickly he determined that they must be the vessel's crew, and that they had been told only that a nameless party occupied the guest

191

room. Their first view of him obviously raised more questions than the master wished to answer. As he firmly shooed them back to their duties, they mumbled over the mystery.

"Good to see you up and about," the master said, leaning down and offering him a hand.

Jonah stood to his feet shakily and stared shamefaced into the Phoenician's skeptical eyes.

"You must be cold," the merchant observed. "It is a brisk day. Go below and get your heaviest cloak."

He was cold. In his rush to leave the hold, he had not thought of the weather. Nodding, he excused himself and slunk back down the stairs.

He still had not asked their destination; and he wondered now how good a seaman he would be.

CHAPTER
3

Jonah was four days into the 2,400-mile trip to Tarshish. When he had learned that, indeed, the ship's ultimate destination was the most westerly port of the Mediterranean world, his heart had sped oddly.

Being accustomed to giving thanks to Jehovah for all his blessings, he had by habit concluded that the Almighty had arranged this good fortune, as well. But the impulse to praise God for the choice of vessels quickly passed, and his spirit blushed as he remembered that it was the Lord himself from whom he ran.

Truly, in his inmost being, he knew the call to Nineveh had been of God. He could not, in good conscience, convince himself that the notion was anything but heaven-sent. If he could have, he would not have been running at all. He would simply have raised a fist to Satan's face and ordered him to be silent.

Amittai had told him that the sons of God had such power, to silence Satan and to calm the devouring lion.

How he missed his father just now, the saintly tentmaker with the calloused fingers and hardened knees. And how he missed Jeroboam, his brother and royal friend!

He stood this afternoon at the stern of the ship, watching the wakes of foam that trailed behind, churned by the steersman's rudders and by the rhythmic oars of galley slaves below. He had not been on the bottom decks where dark-skinned captives, bound to serve a lifetime upon the master's boat, worked the slender oak bats that powered the vessel. But he felt he could sympathize with their plight. For, though he had chosen his passage, he was bound in spirit.

His condition, in fact, was in some ways more to be pitied than theirs. For while a slave of men might still have communion with God, an apostate has nothing but agony of soul.

Nevertheless, at this point he was content to be going to Tarshish. At least there was nothing that could be done to stop him now; and even should he earnestly desire to turn back, there was no reversing the captain's westward movement.

Therefore Jonah was free to experience the grim relief that comes from the knowledge that a decision once acted upon, though criminal, cannot be changed. And were he to seek forgiveness now, surely he would have the fellowship of God, he reasoned, as well as the destiny of his choice.

Though the contemplation of such fellowship seemed less than ideal, he was willing to settle for spiritual mediocrity. After all, was not Jehovah an understanding God? Did he truly wish anything but happiness for his children? Surely in time the trespass would be forgotten, and the Lord would bless him in the path he had taken.

Jonah turned his mind toward Spain, and tried, for the first time since boarding, to enjoy the voyage. How many Gath-hepherites, after all, had ever gone on a pleasure cruise across the world?

He allowed himself to revel in fantasies of exotic ports and foreign women, of wealth beyond imagining in the Land of Copper. He knew that the refinery at Tarshish would not have been surpassed even by the smelters of Solomon.

Surely there was a place of service for him in such a city. God had used him mightily in the past. Was Nineveh the only needy spot on earth?

Jonah left the stern and walked along the deck until he came to the vessel's upturned stem. As he passed shipmen, he smiled, his chin raised despite his rumpled appearance and their dubious expressions.

How glorious it was to be free! he considered, as he leaned over the rail and surveyed the lapis lazuli waters. Spray from the plowing prow ascended in a gentle vapor, caressing his face like a reassuring whisper.

But as he peered through it, his vision was caught by the great eye painted on the vessel's nose. Suddenly a shiver passed down his spine.

Of course it was an illusion, he reasoned. But it seemed the eye observed him. And its assessment of him was anything but kind.

CHAPTER
4

Jonah had never been given to strong drink. But a burden of guilt can do strange things to any man — even to a prophet of God.

Shortly after the voyage had begun, when Jonah had settled into his chamber, the captain provided him, along with his evening meal, a bottle of the fine Syrian wine from the cargo. "Until you have your sea legs," he had said, smiling, "you may find that your stomach objects to the rocking of the ship. This will help calm you."

To Jonah's surprise, he had had little trouble with nausea on the trip. His upset was of a different nature. He was finding that the wine worked wonders to calm that kind of churning, as well. He turned frequently to the pungent tranquilizer as the journey progressed, as each new harbor reminded him of the distance he had put between himself and Israel — between himself and the will of God. He resorted to the sweet sedative to ease his mind's restless drumming and the persistent nagging of his soul.

When the shipmaster checked in on him, he always told him he was keeping closed within his room — with the wineskin — for his stomach's sake.

Day and night ran together in an unbroken continuum. He saw neither the rising nor the setting of the sun. He slept a good deal.

But in his dreamy stupor, peace eluded him. In fact, the haunting visions of Ashurdan and the hounding appeals of Jehovah became hallucinatory, driving him to react in strange and fearsome ways.

No one witnessed his ravings. Oh, there were those crewmen who, passing on the deck overhead, claimed they heard him groaning or wailing. But their fellow sailors assured them it must be the wind or the creaking of the timbers.

No one saw him pound his head against the walls of his little hold, nor did anyone know he spent long hours upon his knees, pleading for respite from his private hell.

But the rumors concerning him were growing more colorful, especially in the eerie hours after sunset and just before dawn, when human beings are prone to their most bizarre imaginings.

By the eighth week at sea, when the ship was coming near Carthage, the seamen had determined that the stranger below, the one who never showed his face, must have an unusually infamous past. His history must be so notorious that even the gods pursued him.

They were used to peculiar people booking passage for very private reasons, to places very distant from their native lands. They were accustomed to encountering the most ignominious of characters upon the sea. But there was no accounting for the sounds of torment that became more audible with each passing night — sounds of bedevilment arising from the pit beneath. Except for assuming they were the floggings of the gods upon the poor fellow's soul, there was no accounting for them.

Nonetheless, Jonah kept to his sanctuary, revealing himself only when he needed more wine. And this he requested more and more often.

The Phoenician colony of Carthage was nearly within sight. At dawn tomorrow, the ship would surely reach its famous shores.

Energy about the vessel was at a peak, as sailors and officers eagerly looked forward to a layover in the entertaining port. Once they had stowed away all the lead and ivory that the master had purchased from traders there, they would be heading into town for three days of merrymaking.

Carthage, coveted for its prime position, jutting into the Great Sea like a beckoning finger and invading the mainstream of traffic east and west, was the favorite stop-off for its founding nationals. Since its beginning, when it was erected by Princess Dido on land secured through trickery from the local Africans, it had been a special trophy. Its original landlord, content to give Dido as much property as an ox hide could cover, had not expected her to order the skin cut into infinitesimal strips and spread end to end as boundary markers. Ever since, the site had evoked a sense of celebration and hilarity among Phoenician sailors, inspiring frivolity and playfulness.

Jonah slept through the heightened activity, which marked the men's preparation for the morrow. They had begun moving cargo from the hold to the deck before moonrise, in anticipation of unloading it early the next morning. By the time dark descended, they were already donning a party mood.

Since they must be alert for work the coming day, they did not abandon all judgment as they passed their flagons and sang their songs. But as the ship plowed the waters, shortening the distance between themselves and the taverns of Carthage, they were determined that nothing would dampen their enthusiasm for the layover.

When the mate who manned the swaying crow's nest climbed the mast for the final time that evening, and when he called down the sighting of a great bank of ominous clouds to windward, no one took much care. Port was only hours away. Surely no brewing storm could catch the vessel before it rested secure on the golden shore.

CHAPTER
5

Worthless! Worthless counselors are you all!" Ashur-dan railed as he paced his elevated stage. The throne room of Nineveh was filled wall to wall with all the wisemen who could be found in the city and its suburbs. The magi who had predicted the plague stood by ashen-faced as their monarch castigated them and their fellow advisors with venomous epithets.

"My kingdom is being eroded away by barbarians on the north, vassals on the coast, and disease within the capital! I am told that I have offended some faceless god of Israel, and now I am threatened by the provincial lords of Palestine with the utter devastation of my empire!"

The veins of the monarch's neck protruded blue and throbbing beneath his flushed skin, and he wielded stabbing glances at the helpless diviners.

"Had I not seen with my own eyes the

fulfillment of your prophecies, I would have you all hanged!" he cried. "And I *shall* have you hanged yet, if you cannot tell me how to appease the deity of the Hebrews."

The spokesman who led the crowd, the eldest of the court seers, raised a tentative hand and cleared his throat. When Ashurdan called on him, he offered weakly, "We have inquired of the priests of Jehovah as to how their god is placated. They do not respond, Your Majesty."

The emperor sighed heavily and traipsed across his platform, having heard it all before.

"We have tried to learn what we can about this 'Jehovah,' or 'Yahweh,'" the sage continued. "Actually, sire, he goes by so many names, the uninformed might suppose the Hebrews have a pantheon of deities."

Ashur-dan stopped his pacing long enough to ask if the Hebrews did not, like other nations, have numerous gods.

"No, indeed, sire," the counselor replied. "They worship only the one, though they call him many things."

At this, the audience of learned thinkers laughed condescendingly, finding the whole notion of a single deity ludicrous, and the application of many names to the one a hypocritical irony. But when the speaker made the next pronouncement, they grew sullen.

"In fact, only a few years ago all shrines and altars to Baal and Astarte, with whom Jehovah once shared his temples, were torn down."

The emperor faced his advisor squarely. "Baal is our Bel, is that not correct? And Astarte is our Ishtar?"

"Yes, Your Majesty."

The imperial overlord clenched his fists, feeling his impotence more keenly than ever.

"Jeroboam did this?" he asked.

"The same," the counselor confirmed.

Ashur-dan was quiet a long while, his gaze lowered and his shoulders sagging.

"Can you tell me nothing of this Hebrew god?" he at last demanded. "Has he no star in the heavens which can be divined? Perhaps a celestial luminary that can be read . . . ?"

The wiseman only shook his head. "We could find no star for Jehovah," he explained. "It seems this being does not speak through the stars. We know nothing of his ways, nor of what can appease him."

Now Ashur-dan grew restless, and locking his fingers together, he gazed over the heads of his audience. "What manner of god is this who comes against us?" he muttered. "What kind of god demands the demise of other deities, yet allows no appeal? What kind of god overthrows the idols of other nations, yet has no form or substance that we may lay our fears at his feet?"

The ruler left his stage and walked to the veranda overlooking his death-struck city. His counselors watched him quietly, having no word of comfort.

"He must be a very bloody god," they heard him say. "Bloodier than all the stars of Nineveh."

Then, with a burst of inspiration, he turned to his advisors, his eyes full of a sad hope. And as he assessed the situation, it was with a trembling heart that he delivered his edict.

"The great god Asshur, when he is very angry, is satisfied with only one thing."

The listeners looked at one another fearfully, shaking their heads and conferring together in dread.

"If the plague be not lifted within six weeks, and if Nineveh yet stands," the king commanded, "the firstborn of every family shall be brought to the city square. . . . Perhaps Jehovah will be appeased by their blood."

"But, sire, are you certain . . . ?" the eldest objected.

"What I have spoken, I have spoken," Ashur-dan replied.

CHAPTER
6

The dense bank of iron-gray clouds that the mate had spied from the crow's nest was closing in on the Carthage-bound ship at an alarming rate. No one aboard had anticipated the speed with which the storm would hit.

With the oncoming clouds, the sea was lashed and swirled, whipped by an eerie despondent wind, and the boat began to reel like a drunkard upon the waves.

Most of the men, still convinced that they would make port by morning, expected that even though the sudden gale was a phenomenon, it would quickly pass and a clear sky would follow the freakish onslaught.

But soon it became apparent that this was no passing breeze. Where there had been stars visible in a pristine heaven, a shroud of fog interposed itself. And within moments a full-scale tempest surrounded the ship.

Now fear filled the crew's sea-hardened hearts. As the black night waters reached ominous hands into the vessel, the boat leaned awkwardly. "We'll be swamped!" someone cried. "Give her ballast!"

Instantly the sailors began to adjust the load upon the deck floor, scooting bundles and barrels to the higher side, in the hope that redistributed weight would level the ship. But the situation only grew more precarious, as even the elevated side was grasped by the sea.

The captain, who had been sleeping soundly throughout the sailors' previous revelry, had wakened the instant the wind began to blow. Like a mother, ever alert to the slightest cry of her child, he had bolted from bed the moment the craft began to totter, and he pressed now along the deck rail, studying the blustering waters and buckling timbers with the eye of experience.

The owner, joining him, peered wildly about the boat, watching the crewmen in their mad scrambles. "We're breaking up!" he shouted. And directing the captain's attention to the hull, he pointed to a length of cypress sheathing hanging loose and flopping in the water.

The captain began barking commands in rapid succession, ordering the steersman to appoint an assistant so that the rudders of each quarter might be manned simultaneously, and then crying for the anchors to be lowered.

Instantly, strong arms cranked away at the capstans, sending the immense, flat-pronged weights plummeting to the sea floor.

"Take on help!" he cried again, giving the most feared order in the sailing language.

Without hesitation, the well-trained seamen began to haul cables and chains out of bolted lockers, which ringed the deck. As the ship strained at the seams, the crew tugged and hoisted the heavy implements, looping them over the width of the vessel and passing them underneath the hull in several places by means of long dragging cords. The feat required many hands, and could involve the actual diving of swimmers to facilitate the maneuver, should the girdles become snarled. All was accomplished with dexterity, however, and the chains were tightened against the invading waters, which already threatened the craft's lower quadrants.

Still, the ship bolted upon the teeming

waves, and cries from the galley betrayed the mounting fear that the oarsmen fought. Several of their long oaken paddles had been broken to splinters by the hammering sea, and the men below were thrown against one another upon their cramped benches, creating bedlam. Though their governor tried to keep control, the task overwhelmed him. Presently, as the slaves began to cry out for their lives, he unlocked their shackles and allowed them to fend for themselves.

Soon the top deck was swarming with humanity, sailors and officers lost among frightened natives who had not seen the open air for months.

As the captain continued to shout his commands, and the owner watched the mania which could never save his ship, sailors began to throw the cargo overboard, in hopes that lighter weight might keep the vessel afloat. Already the lowest deck was flooding, and it would be only a matter of time before the entire structure floundered.

Bolts of Phoenician purple were toppled into the deep, their dyes blending quickly with the opaque waters; and large flasks of perfumed oil were shattered, spreading their contents in a greasy sheen across the waves. Cartons of burlap-wrapped wine bottles crashed against bobbing mummy cases — but the dreaming likenesses of Egyptian noblemen etched upon the lids did not awaken.

As the storm grew more ferocious, its voice a demanding wail, sailors fell to their knees, crying out to the many deities of their various towns, invoking the favor of Melkart, if they were from Tyre; Eshmun of Sidon; or, as matters worsened, the father of the Phoenician pantheon, El. Of course, the names of Baal, his son, and Astarte, the most popular *baalath*, were sprinkled liberally throughout each prayer. And joining with these petitions were the cries of the African slaves, appealing to the numerous tribal gods they carried in their hearts, despite the white man's influence.

A wild chorus the frantic ravings made, ascending into the storm but not breaking it. As the elements raged, it became difficult to discern the intonations of prayer from the mocking of the wind.

Somehow, in the midst of this madness, the owner realized that Jonah was nowhere to be seen among the hysterical crew. In fact, he had not come up from the hold since the storm began.

And somehow, despite the distraction of

the scene before him, he sensed that Jonah's presence aboard figured in the desperate plight of the vessel.

Grasping the captain by the sleeve, he demanded his assistance.

"Go below and find the Hebrew!" he cried.

The pilot, studying him as though he had lost his mind, shook his head. "We cannot worry over a passenger now!" he protested.

"It is the ship I worry over!" the owner barked. "Your legs are more sure than mine. Go below and find the man!"

The captain, seeing that he could not dissuade the master, reluctantly turned for the trapdoor. Surely the Hebrew had already drowned in his cabin or been crushed beneath the storeroom's buckled timbers.

But there was nothing to be done on deck. Taking with him the only lantern aboard that had not been doused by wind or water, he stumbled toward the ship's dank belly, and hoped some god went with him.

CHAPTER
7

The captain made his way, at great risk, down the wobbly ladder leading to the guest chamber. Loosened from their bolts by the bucking sea, the stairs gave with each step he took, and when he reached the deck beneath, he found it necessary to duck his head to avoid the beams that sagged precariously overhead.

The hold was empty, having been cleared of cargo the night before. Nothing blocked his passage, and fears that the Hebrew may have been crushed beneath some fallen timber were relieved as he found the storeroom intact. Were the guest still alive, however, he could not imagine why he would not have joined his panicked neighbors above.

Hesitating only a moment, he knocked loudly on the compartment door, and, receiving no answer, was more certain than ever that the passenger had not survived the storm's first onslaught. Supposing that Jonah had been thrown from bed, probably breaking his neck, the captain lifted the latch with shaky fingers.

The door opened on a smelly, disheveled room. The pilot held his sleeve to his nose and peered in, wondering if indeed the one who had dwelt here might have been deceased for some time before the storm.

Thrusting his lantern into the dank chamber, he saw, among the toppled furnishings and trays of uneaten food, countless wineskins, which the "seasick" guest had apparently tossed aside in one stupor after another.

Then, he found him.

An unmoving mound, still slung in the hammock, told him that Jonah had not risen since the tempest began.

The captain, who revered all superstitions of the sea, did not like to think that a paying passenger had died aboard his vessel. It did not bode well. Perhaps, in truth, this had been the cause of the freakish gale.

Stumbling from the room, he started for the stairs. He was about to order the corpse buried honorably in the deep, that the death cloud might be lifted, when a low groan from the chamber drew him back.

Surely it was only the creaking of the hold, he told himself. When it came again, clearly issuing from the lump upon the hammock, he shuddered.

Carefully he approached the swaying cradle, and bracing himself against the wall, peeked in at the Hebrew. "Are you ill?" he whispered, his heart in his throat.

Jonah seemed to respond, turning over on his sling, his eyes still firmly shut.

"I say, are you ill?" the captain repeated.

When the passenger only smacked his lips lazily in slumber, bearing an insipid smile upon his drowsy face, the pilot grew angry. Shaking Jonah by the shoulders, he dislodged another wineskin, which the Hebrew had cradled in drunken oblivion all through the raging storm. As the bottle toppled from the bunk, spilling its remaining contents upon the captain's cloak, the officer was outraged.

"Why, you are nothing but a sot!" he shouted. "How is it that you are sleeping?" Grabbing the prophet by the arms, he lifted him from his nest and flung him to the floor.

"Get up!" he demanded, glaring down at the fugitive with contemptuous eyes. "Do you not hear the shrieking wind? Do you not hear the cries of the men above? Call on your god! Perhaps *he* can save us!"

Jonah rose to his knees, holding his head in his hands, trying to clear his vision. But the pilot had no patience. Grasping him again by the cloak, he jerked him to his feet and chucked his chin erect with two strong fingers. "Look alive, man!" he growled. "The master sent me below to save you, though I cannot imagine why. Now you'll go above with me, or I'll surely leave you here for the sea to swallow!"

At this the captain dragged him up the stairs. When he reached the trap door, he had barely lifted it an inch before the gale tore it from his fingers, ripping it open, as if the sky itself demanded Jonah be sent forth. As the two men made the top deck, the Hebrew slumping against the pilot with an aching head and churning stomach, the wind howled more ominously than ever.

The crewmen were strangely quiet, gathered together near the helm, intent on some activity within their tight circle. The dark slaves, ringing the ship rail, still called upon their gods, beating upon their heads, their breasts, and their thighs, and shouting in their native tongues the names of jungle deities.

No one seemed to notice the two who had just emerged from the hold; or if they did, they cared nothing for them.

When the master saw the pilot dragging Jonah to the cluster of sailors, he hurried to him. "So, he is still with us!" he cried, seeing that the passenger was alive after all. "Hurry! We are casting lots!"

Assisting the captain with the obstinate cargo, the master lifted Jonah by the arm and helped tow him to the helm. "Here!" he commanded, getting the huddle's attention. "While you're at it, make a plug for this one!"

Jonah, tossed to the deck floor, sprawled indecorously before the gaze of his fellow seamen. The bitter cold and the lashing air were reviving him; and presently, he rose again to his knees, wiping the stupor from his face.

Despite his foggy head, he quickly discerned that the men were engaged in one of the most common practices of the day, attempting to determine, by the casting of lots, who aboard might be the cause of the ship's ill fortune. It was firmly held, among all societies, that when any calamity descended, it could be traced to an offense given the gods by some mortal. Especially upon the sea, where men were so at the mercy of the elements, the notion was upheld.

On the floor, in the midst of the cloistered group, lay a sitella — a glass jar con-
taining little plugs of wood floating in seawater. The bottle had a neck so narrow
that, when turned upside down, only one
counter could escape at a time. Each man
on board, from slave to officer, was represented by a plug; and it was believed that
the emerging piece would reveal the criminal.

The master had just reminded them of
the passenger's presence on ship. There
was no counter in the bottle for Jonah. He
shuddered now, as one sailor took a pen-
knife and began to whittle "Hebrew" upon
a small piece of decking.

The crew muttered among themselves in
private whispers, eyeing Jonah as his plug
was forced into the sitella. And the two
officers who had dragged him forth held
him firmly on either side.

As the bottle was shaken, its contents
dancing like noose-hung men, excitement
grew. The sailors began to chant again to
their gods, joining their voices with those
of the slaves who cavorted madly about
the deck. The wind itself and the rocking
ship could not quiet them. Nor could the
spilling sea, which repeatedly washed their
ankles, drown their determination to

identify the culprit.

When at last the one in charge tipped the bottle down, and removed his thumb from its mouth, allowing a single wet plug to poke forth its head, a hush came over the crew. Drawing it out, the sailor turned it over carefully, then lifted his eyes to the master.

"Hold it up!" the owner cried. As the fellow complied, every man present could read the designation.

Suddenly there was a unanimous shout, and the crowd lunged as one body toward Jonah. But the master called them off, and they stood back, teeth bared and hands clenched.

Jonah slumped again to the floor, burying his head in his fists, and weeping sorely.

Though the men would honor their master, they would not be silenced. "Tell us now!" they cried, directing their questions to the passenger. "Why has this calamity struck? Who are you? Where do you come from? What is your occupation?"

One after another the demands tumbled forth, until Jonah's ears ached with the weight of them.

"I . . . I am a Hebrew . . . ," he answered weakly.

"This we know!" they shouted. "What is your crime?"

"My God is Jehovah . . . Lord God of heaven who made the sea and dry land," he added, hoping that such prattle might appease them.

"Yes . . . yes!" they cried. "All Hebrews worship Jehovah. But there is more! What is your crime?"

The master, seeing that his lads would not be held off much longer, but were bent on tearing the passenger to shreds, leaned over him anxiously.

"Speak, man! We all know you are hiding something," he pleaded. "We have known it from the beginning! Now would you see us all die, for your sake?"

The fugitive, knowing that he could deny his condition no longer, sighed deeply and confessed, "I was given a commission by my God, and I chose instead to flee him. Thus I came on board your ship. And now, he pursues me to the sinking of this vessel!"

As the import of Jonah's words struck them, the men became more frightened than ever. "How could you do this?" they railed. "No man can escape his god!"

And as they again moved toward him, the master intervened. "Think, lads!" he commanded. "What greater ill might come upon us at the hands of this man's god if we touch a hair of his head!"

Falling back, the sailors consulted among themselves, certain that their demise was imminent no matter which way they turned.

As the waters grew increasingly violent, the owner, hovering again over Jonah, demanded his cooperation. "What should we do to you that the sea may become calm for us?" he asked. "What does your god require?"

The Hebrew, overcome with guilt and with the burden of the Lord's hand upon his soul, cried out with a rasping voice, his arms flung open in surrender, "Pick me up and throw me into the sea! Then it will become calm. For I know that on account of me this great storm has come upon you."

Casting himself face first upon the deck, he allowed the full impact of his crime to sweep over him. Throaty sobs wrenched him, and he regarded not the looks of disgust and outrage passed between his companions.

"What are we waiting for?" someone shouted. "We have heard his sentence, given at his own hand! Let's take him!"

Once again, the crowd moved to lay hold of Jonah, but the owner would not permit them. As the waters swelled more convulsively than ever, he was convinced the ship would be sunk by the Hebrew's god if he were harmed by alien hands.

"Get below!" he cried. "Each man to the oars! And take the slaves with you! We will spare our vessel, though a thousand criminals board her! But we will take no man's life!"

The captain looked at the master as though he were mad. But by all the rules of the sea, which he loved with his whole heart, he could never sanction a mutiny. So he, too, commanded his men to the galley.

One by one the crew complied, staggering down the splintered stairs, past the hold and into the viscera of the ship. But no sooner had the lowest deck been entered, than it began to fill dangerously with water. For hours the sea had threatened that quarter, invading it in small rivulets along the bituminous seams. Now great gushes of foamy liquid washed through the deck, forcing the men to turn around and give up their mission.

Joining their fellow seamen on the second galley, they took up oars alongside slave and mate, and each did his best to hold the ship erect.

For an hour they rowed, desperately seeking the coast of Carthage. But the sea only grew more obstinate, and when the second galley began to fill with brine, they were forced to abandon it as well.

Everyone was topside once more. There had been no mutiny, only the rebellion of the elements. And the master and the captain were obliged to accept the inevitable.

Looking at one another, hoping against hope that there might be another way, they at last lifted Jonah to his feet and stared up into the howling sky.

It was proper that the captain should deliver the final appeal. He had never before spoken to Jehovah, but he did it with the grace of one experienced in the ways of many cultures:

"We earnestly pray, O Lord, do not let us perish on account of this man's life. And do not put innocent blood upon us. For thou, O Lord, hast done as thou hast pleased."

Then the two officers picked up their passenger, lifting his feet off the deck. Jonah's eyes were wide, but he said not a word, nor did he struggle, as they took him to the rail.

Quickly, not allowing themselves to

think twice, they cast him overboard.

And just as quickly, the sea stopped its raging, and all the elements were calm.

CHAPTER
8

It was night again on the Great Sea. Jonah had been treading water all day, clinging fearfully to a slippery piece of flotsam, one of the mummy cases thrown overboard during the storm.

A grisly savior it was, this wooden sarcophagus. The sleeping face etched into the lid and the hands folded in endless slumber only reminded him, each time he looked upon them, of the fragility of life and the hopelessness of his own situation.

In the dark, his life preserver was especially gruesome, joined as it was by its bobbing fellows — other coffins hungry for corpses they would never cradle. All about the nearby waters the containers drifted, many far out from the ship, having been dispersed atop the waves like discarded memorials. The expensive boxes had not been unloaded at any Egyptian port, and Jonah wondered now what African lords would have found them useful. He remembered that the Egyptians had consuls stationed in diverse corners of the map. Doubtless these coffins had been intended for a multiple funeral, perhaps for the family of some Carthaginian diplomat.

It little mattered for whom whey were meant. When a man's life was over, it was of little consequence whether he was buried on a marble slab or a pine board.

An orange glow dappled the brine near Jonah's slimy barge — the light of a sacrificial fire that had burned aboard the merchant ship since the storm abated. The pyre was in honor of Jehovah, and a small sea bird had been offered upon it in gratitude to the Hebrew god who had spared the Phoenician vessel. The sailors and officers had fallen to their knees, paying homage and vows to the foreign deity the moment the sea had calmed. Then they had set up a chant, one based upon some pagan song, but calling out thanks to the god of Israel.

Even now the minor chords of the seamen's harmony drifted across the waters, adding a strange note of irony to Jonah's despair. He would never sing again, he knew. He would never offer up sacrifices in the hallowed halls of Israel. The only gift he could bring was the doubtful largess of his own death, which this very moment provoked praise for Yahweh from the lips of Gentiles.

Ha! he thought, casting his gaze toward the star-flecked heavens. *So you have had your way after all, my Lord! I am a missionary despite my every rebellion, winning for you the hearts of pagan dogs, though I never set foot in Nineveh!*

The cold sea seemed to swell in response to Jonah's mocking, and as he glanced fearfully at his companions, the silent cartons of death, they appeared to multiply. It was insane to imagine so, he knew, but he thought he heard them whisper as they clattered now and then against one another.

And it seemed they watched him, though their eyes were closed. In fact, the sea was full of faces. And as he shook his head, the sailors' chorus spilling in eerie echoes across the waves, the ship's prow seemed to study him, its own gigantic eyes motionless and haunting.

Jonah did not know what time it was when the coffin slipped from his grasp, leaving him to flounder alone. He was asleep when the hollow raft slithered from his arms and rode out of reach. It was only when he took in a mouthful of water that he awoke to imminent drowning.

Shaking himself violently, he tried to forestall panic and take stock of his situation.

Though the heavens were still dark and glowering, though a heavy mist rose from the sea, he could tell it was near morning, for the clouds were tinged with coral in the east. He could discern no silhouette of the ship across the waves, however, and knew he had drifted far from the sliver of hope which that sight had evoked.

With mounting apprehension he struggled to keep himself afloat until he could find another "life buoy" to cling to. He wriggled his limbs desperately in an attempt to keep his blood circulating. The water near the African shore was warmer than that farther off coast, but still he was nearly numb with cold; and in the darkness he had to touch his legs to know they were still attached.

A sharp wind had descended from the north, and adding to the fatigue that he already fought were the challenges of a rocking sea and demanding billows.

Though he had earlier managed to stay alive by cleaving to the sarcophagus, such an effort now demanded more energy than he could muster. He found that, left to the mercy of the water, his remaining strength was quickly dissipating. As the waves passed over him again and again, slamming his body like a massive hammer, he tried in vain to keep his head above the surface.

Repeatedly now he found himself sinking, clawing his way toward daylight and air, only to be pushed beneath the choppy line where oxygen was inaccessible and where the lungs strained against its loss.

When he could manage to take in a breath, he wheezed helplessly, "I am cast out of thy sight! Forsake me not utterly!"

But there was no reply. Sea and sky were silent, and he was alone upon the waters. There was no more castaway cargo to which he could cling. In his solitude he imagined he and the sea were becoming one, that it was invading his very soul as it invaded his body.

As he struggled, however, he perceived with his nearly unfeeling arms the presence of something nearby. It seemed to be reaching for him, its long, slimy tendrils ready to encompass his limbs.

Jonah's pulse raced, and his heart pounded. Visions of some gigantic octopus or terrifying and unnamed monster leaped to mind, and he began flailing in an attempt to flee the fearsome grappler.

But the pursuer was too close. The more he tried to work away from its grasping tentacles, the more entwined he became in its bulbous net.

When its weblike arms began to encircle his head, wrapping about his face and tugging at his neck, he cried aloud. But he quickly determined to keep his mouth closed, as water filled his throat.

Suddenly, he was pulled under. Down, down the faceless enemy dragged him, and the more he fought its pull, the more it adhered, weaving mucousy ropes into a tangle about his legs.

How long he fell, he could not determine. At last he was being yanked along a rocky floor until his captor suddenly lurched, as if caught on something.

Jonah could not contain his breath another moment. Desperately he reached through the slithery knot which held one arm, and he waved his hand back and forth, trying to grasp whatever had attached itself to his host.

A shot of pain raced up from his fingers, and he jerked his hand back. He could not see that it was bleeding badly, but he knew

it had scraped against some spiny object —
and, despite his fear, he reached out again.

He and his predator were imprisoned in
a bank of razor-sharp coral.

"Lord God, I surrender!" he groaned,
expelling his chest full of air in a great
bubble.

His soul fainted, all strength escaping
with the exhaled orb which now floated
toward the surface. But just as oblivion
was about to overtake him, daylight — or
some form of light — permeated the
depths. And with his last conscious perception, the sight of two great eyes advancing
on him filled his senses.

"The ship!" he marveled in delirium.
"The ship returns for me!"

Then darkness, like the grave, consumed
him. And the Angel of Death was at hand.

CHAPTER
9

If thought were possible in the grave, Jonah was thinking. He had opened his eyes on impenetrable darkness, and feeling was slowly returning to his extremities.

"Lord God . . . ," he whispered, "can the dead perceive their own condition?"

He lay still for a long time, trying to interpret the peculiar sensation of being hurtled feet first through a long tunnel.

No — not *through* a tunnel, but within and by means of it — as though the tunnel itself moved, carrying him . . . he knew not where.

He rested upon his stomach, his arms curled fetally to his breast; and as he dared to reach forth a tentative finger, he prodded the floor upon which he reposed. To his amazement, he could still feel the entwining cords of the captor which had dragged him beneath the sea — the tentacles of the nameless creature that had bound his head and limbs. Failing to make sense of this, he analyzed the substance of his bed, and found it even more of a mystery.

The floor of the grave was warm and . . . fleshy. It was, in fact, soft to the touch and very moist.

Taking courage to lean upon one elbow, he proceeded to investigate the walls and ceiling of his tomb, finding it all of like material.

This is no sea cave! he marveled. Nor was it the hold of the phantom ship he had supposed he saw just before life escaped him.

The prophet, once the privileged guardian of uncanny insights, lay down in utter confusion, unable to decipher the simplest aspect of his surroundings. But then the world of the dead was a dimension that no man understood until his time had come, he reasoned. He could not prepare himself for it by any previous experience.

As his faculties grew clearer, however, he became increasingly uncomfortable. He reached up to pry the tendrils of the parasite from off his face, and found, to his surprise, that they could be unfastened. Apparently the creature had not regained its ability to move, as he had. Perhaps sub-human entities never did revive within the tomb, he posited.

As his sense of touch returned, so did the pang of cuts he had received from the coral reef. There was nothing that his eyes could appreciate in the black hold, and there was no sound discernible.

But Jonah's most acute perception, besides the pain, was of a foul odor permeating his house of death. That least perfected of his human senses, the olfactory, was strongly aroused by the nauseating stench. And Jonah, who like most men had generally ignored that fifth faculty, was overcome.

He remembered how the tombs of Israel were sealed, and why the dead were bound with spices. Apparently, the company within this sepulcher had not received such tender care. *He* certainly had not.

He wondered who else might occupy this chamber. But even as he questioned, his mind, like his other powers, began to clear.

What was he thinking? There were no graves upon the bottom of the sea! If a man lost his life to the waters, he became no more than flotsam — or, waterlogged, sank to the floor like a rock.

Yet here he found himself encompassed by some kind of warm cradle, one almost of . . . flesh and blood . . . a container that seemed to be moving, to have vitality of its own.

The grave had no life, neither did it preserve life!

And a dead man did *not* think! Not until he rested in paradise, or burned in . . .

Yes . . . that was it. *Perhaps this was Hades*, the realm of the damned.

Jonah's soul sank within him. He surely was a candidate for hell. If any man deserved the wrath of God, it was he.

Hot tears poured down his cheeks, and his shoulders shook with wracking sobs. "O Lord!" he cried. "Were it possible for a man to return from the grave. . . . O God! If I might only live again, I would never disobey! Never, my Lord!"

Even as he spoke, the foolishness of his petition caused him to blush. Yet still he continued to plead, rocking to and fro, his arms raised to the ceiling of his vault.

Once more, however, a flash of insight illumined the faulty corners of his logic. Hell was a place of torment. Yet the space in which he found himself was, despite its foul aroma, cozy and secure. The only pain he endured arose from scrapes and bruises

— and from mental anguish.

Quickly he began to analyze the bits of information available to him. Raising a hesitant hand, he investigated the creature that had pulled him to the sea floor. It seemed nothing more than a tangle of cold rope, marked here and there by leafy appendages and ball-shaped bladders.

Weeds! he reckoned. *Seaweed!*

Madly now, he knelt upright, surveying the walls and ceiling of his berth.

But just as he shifted his position, his knees boring into his soft bed, the persistent thrust of his carrier seemed to slow. As if in response to Jonah's altered posture, the whole house of death lurched to a stop, its propelling motion being replaced by a gentle swaying.

The inmate froze, fearful to move again, lest the dungeon shake violently.

To this point there had been no sound discernible. But with this stilling, the silence became more keen, interrupted only by peculiar sloshings and gurglings.

Jonah's heart raced. "Lord," he whispered, "I am trapped within the belly of some monster!"

Sinking down again upon his soft pallet, he quaked with a mixture of emotions. He had reason for joy. After all, he was alive!

But how could a man survive such a predicament?

Surely God in heaven knew where he was. But Jonah could not see his saving hand.

Leaning against the moist wall of the creature's maw, the renegade prophet trembled. He drew his knees to his chin, and stared wide-eyed into a darkness far denser than death.

CHAPTER
10

There was no accounting for time in the belly of the sea creature. In total darkness, Jonah could measure neither night nor day. The only event to transpire with enough regularity to allow a rough estimation of the hours was the monster's ingestion of food.

That the Hebrew was indeed embodied within the maw of an animal was confirmed to him the first time the being opened its enormous mouth to overtake an unwary school of fish. Instantly a swell of cold water rushed down the creature's gullet, swamping the prophet, and leaving only a small pocket of air at the top of the cavity.

Panicked, he grappled for oxygen along the mucousy ceiling until the waters subsided, spewn out through the gigantic, tooth-lined orifice.

Jonah could see just far enough up the purple throat to catch a glimpse of daylight. And as he found his footing again, sliding into a knee-deep pool of wriggling carp, it occurred to him that he was nothing more than fodder — a nighttime snack — just as the fish were the monster's breakfast.

He had considered attempting to burrow his way toward freedom up the slippery gullet. But such imaginings were prior to his sighting of the terrible teeth that barred the way.

"Leviathan!" he groaned. This was no ordinary fish. It was a warm-blooded man-eater, one of the species designated by the Hebrews as "monstrosities of the deep."

With the glimpse of daylight, he knew he had been within the whale's belly at least one entire night. And the flash of illumination, which the open mouth afforded, described to him the nature of his position.

He rested upon a fold or ridge of the whale's maw — perhaps the ledge imposed by a rib, or simply a pucker in the stomach lining. The animal was so enormous that the tongue alone, he clearly noted, was the size of an elephant! That he had not already been digested by potent acids was due to the fact that he had landed upon this little niche, tucked away from the dissolving liquid.

He did discern a tingling on his skin, however; evidence that the inhospitable chamber would ultimately have its way with him.

Air was sparse in his mucousy nest. He dare not take it for granted. Ever since waking, he had been light-headed; and he realized that he had survived during his comatose state because his bodily processes had been slowed. He had heard of such phenomena occurring for those who should have lost their lives trapped beneath water or in accidents at sea.

Fearing to shift from the secure space that he had been afforded lest he slip into the stomach's abyss, he hugged the wall to his back and tried to remember words of faith his father had taught him. Phrases from childhood meditations and traditional Hebrew psalms rose from the rich storehouse of his privileged training. And between them he wove the particulars of his circumstances, as was common for an Israelite at prayer.

"I cried by reason of my affliction unto the Lord," he whispered, "and he heard me. Out of the belly of hell cried I, and you heard my voice.

"For you had cast me into the deep, in the midst of the seas. And the floods com-

240

passed me about. All your billows and your waves passed over me.

"Then I said, 'I am cast out of your sight.' Yet I will look again toward your holy temple."

Jonah bowed to the darkness and shivered with the hope that his words pierced through the prison walls.

"The waters compassed me about, even to the soul," he continued. "The depth closed me round about, the weeds were wrapped about my head.

"I went down to the bottoms of the mountains; the earth with her bars was about me forever. Yet have you brought up my life from corruption, O Lord my God.

"When my soul fainted within me I remembered the Lord. And my prayer came in unto you, into your holy temple."

The prophet took a hesitant breath, trying to spare the oxygen, as tears poured down his face. His spirit broke, and for a long moment he could say nothing. Then at last he ended with the traditional confession of the repentant: "They that observe lying vanities forsake their own mercy," he cried. "But I will sacrifice unto you with the voice of thanksgiving. I will pay that which I have vowed."

Yes. He was determined. Should the

Lord see fit to rescue him, he would not hesitate to perform his mission. He would go to Nineveh. Indeed, he would go!

But what chance was there that he could survive? What foolishness was this, that he should even ask for such a thing?

Jonah's chin sank to his breast, and a resigned sigh escaped him. Something in his soul, however, would not let go of hope.

"Salvation is of the Lord . . . ," he whispered once more.

And as the black silence cradled him, the gruesome reality of his condition was suppressed. Even his sleep was dreamless, and time was immaterial.

PART FOUR

PURGATORY

*Who in the days of
his flesh, when he had
offered up prayers
and supplications
with strong crying
and tears unto him
that was able to save
him from death, and
was heard . . . though
he were a Son, yet
learned he obedience
by the things which
he suffered. . . .*

HEBREWS 5:7, 8

CHAPTER
1

The next time Jonah awoke, it was to the sound of a great rush and roar. His pallet heaved, and he was thrust toward the ceiling.

He opened his eyes on darkness, and prepared for an onslaught of seawater, expecting that his host had come upon another school of fish.

What he could not have known, since he had been asleep for two full days and nights — and indeed was into his third day in the monster's belly — was that the creature had ingested countless meals since last Jonah gained consciousness. For the whale was a perpetual glutton, sweeping up tons of food each twenty-four-hour period.

The Hebrew braced his feet against the soft floor of his bed, leaning into the wall. But no daylight invaded the cell; neither did a briny wave overwash him. For a long moment there was no further movement on the monster's part, and Jonah wondered if he had dreamed the peculiar upheaval.

But soon enough the spasm repeated itself, thrusting him up the whale's gullet. He barely had time to fear what was happening; and as he lay for a split second upon the creature's tongue, the mouth suddenly opened, revealing the arched orifice leading down into the maw from which he had just ascended. Daylight flooded the cavity, and with one more mighty belch, the whale spewed him forth, hurtling him several hundred feet onto dry shore.

The north African sun blinded him as he lay, pain-wracked, amid a mountain of bile and ambergris. He sat up, bruised from the fall, aching from his three days' captivity, and shielding his vision against the glare of the noonday sun.

As his eyes adjusted to the brilliance of white sand and blue sky, he scanned the waters with a trembling heart. Yes — there it was; the mammoth carnivore that had rescued him from certain death.

Strange that he should view the whale in such terms, he thought. But then God's ways were the ways of irony, Amittai had often declared. And Hebrew humor was punctuated with unexpected twists.

Despite scrapes and the raw sensitivity of acidic skin, Jonah found himself laughing. He sat amid the weeds and the skeletons of lesser animals.

Leviathan rested on the waves, watching him for some time; and Jonah studied the eyes that had reminded him of the Phoenician ship just before his swoon. They seemed very small now against the monster's sweeping skull. But if it were possible for such an animal to show feeling, Jonah was certain he saw a glimmer of sympathetic laughter in the shiny orbs.

The prophet at last struggled upright on shaky legs and peeled the entwining cords of ever-present seaweed from his torso. He then surveyed his location and wondered in which direction to begin his homeward trek, pondering how he should survive another adventure.

But once more, hilarity filled his breast. Jehovah was a very determined God, and Jonah knew that somehow he would yet see the eastern coast . . . and Nineveh.

As he made his way up the beach, he turned another glance seaward. The whale still rested its colossal form upon the bobbing waters. And as Jonah looked on, it spewed from its spout an enormous flume of white brine. Then, humping its back, it dove slick as an eel beneath the surface.

With a flick of its fan-shaped tail, it was gone, its appointed mission complete — just as the prophet's was only beginning.

CHAPTER
2

Jonah was glad for the dark of the Egyptian night. The African sun upon his raw, bleached skin had been nearly unbearable for the past several days of his journey.

Just as his entire sea epic and its aftermath had been fraught with irony, however, even now his peculiar looks — white and ghostly — had served to expedite this trip east.

The first afternoon ashore, having bathed quickly in the stinging brine, he had made his way into a small port town; and not knowing the language, he had been incapable of explaining his fantastic appearance. His foreign dialect, along with his unusual blue eyes, had only added to the illusion that he was a supernatural being. And the dark-skinned villagers, Nubians and assorted Egyptian fishermen, greeted his entrance with awe and fascination.

As word had spread of the phantom's visitation, curiosity turned to superstitious fear. Suspecting some kind of judgment on their humble town, the citizens had gathered about him with gifts: ripe figs and pomegranates, grapes from their private arbors, and salted seafood. Children had strewn his way with desert flowers, and old women had cast golden rings at his feet.

He knew they were trying to appease him — to forestall whatever chastisement he might bring from the gods. He tried to convince them that he was but a man, and that he intended no ill. But it was no use. The more he expostulated in his native tongue, motioning toward the sea or making gestures to describe the whale and its great mouth, the more he convinced them that he was the herald of evil tidings. As he enacted his story, they saw it as a description of their own demise; and they watched his frantic hands and listened to his rapid speech with mounting dread.

Shaking his head, he refused their offerings. But his rejection only incited their fears. With greater fervor they appealed to him, thrusting their finest garments upon his shoulders and forcing their meager wealth into his arms.

At sunset they had watched him leave

their village, stoop-shouldered, his hands laden with rings, his arms with bracelets, and his feet shod with magnificent, tooled sandals. They had sung songs as he departed, glad that he had accepted their sacrifices but praying that he not return.

Once out of their sight, Jonah had sat beneath a wayside grove, stuffing his gold trinkets into a silken satchel, peeling off three royal robes, and rolling them into a neat bundle for his knapsack.

Nearly ill with fatigue, he had slept in the oasis until noon the next day, unable to appreciate the good fortune onto which he had stumbled.

He would appreciate it soon enough, however. Without the intervention of the villagers, he would have been destitute. When he found that he was able to purchase sustenance and walk across the land in style, he began to rediscover the mercy of God.

Tonight he basked beneath a cool moon, his ravaged flesh on the mend. The acidic sting that had begun in the whale's maw was relieved somewhat at evening, though it had, of late, been exchanged for an itching sensation, persistent and aggravating.

Uncomfortable as the prickling irritation

could be, however, it was evidence of healing. And as a fine, scaly scab replaced the rawness, he knew that in time his olive complexion would return, and he would pass for human once again.

Jonah rested upon his back, his hands beneath his head as he studied a desert hawk crossing the moon's face, pursuing the eastern horizon. It reminded him of Assyria, strong and deadly, determined as an archer's arrow.

He wondered if Jehovah had created the Dog of the East, and if he loved it as he must love all works of his own hands. The prophet's head swam with the mystery of God's design — that he alone raised kings and lowered them, and that even the evil ones flourished only at his will.

He watched as the hawk took a sudden dive for some small, helpless creature, invisible to all save his specially keen eyes, and the Hebrew's heart surged.

He hated the killing bird, as he hated Nineveh. Yet he admired its skill and its divinely endowed powers.

"But even the hawk is vulnerable," he whispered, vengeance in his fist. "God gave him wings, and God can break his pinions."

Suddenly, the air about the prophet's

sandy bed swelled with intangible urgency. As if the Lord were impatient with his analysis, he spoke, dartlike, to Jonah's heart:

"Arise! Go to Nineveh, that Great City, and preach unto it the words that I give you!"

Thus rest ended for the night. It would be many hours and miles before he stopped again.

CHAPTER
3

Jonah had not worn the cloak of Amos since he stood atop the Damascus wall during the siege that had given Ben-Hadad's kingdom to Israel.

Throughout the young prophet's ministry he had reserved the garment for the most special occasions, wearing at other times the fine clothes provided by Jeroboam's kindness. Though the old mantle was tattered and worn, it was revered as a sacred vestment; and neither king nor holy man ever suggested it be mended or cleaned. It remained in the same condition as when it was presented to the tentmaker's son, though perhaps a bit more threadbare with use; yet to repair it would have constituted sacrilege, both agreed.

Because it had not been fitting for Jonah to wear it when he had left the palace, he had stored it upon a hook in his chamber, where it awaited his return like a patient shadow.

Sometimes, since no word had been heard from the prophet for weeks, Jeroboam would step secretly into Jonah's quarters, gazing sadly and urgently upon the cloak — as though it might reveal when its owner would come home. It was a foolish hope, he knew. But the simple act of being in the seer's chamber brought a hollow quiet to his soul.

No one in Israel knew where Jonah was. Jeroboam had sent numerous appeals throughout the land. "Locate the prophet," he commanded. Scouting parties had been commissioned. Even old Amittai had been warned that if he knew anything at all of his son's whereabouts, and if he for some reason were hiding information, he could be in danger of royal retribution.

Amittai knew nothing. He had not even known that Jonah had once been headed for Gath-hepher. Before the flight to the sea, the prophet had intended to make his visit a surprise.

Jeroboam was in dire need of guidance — the kind that only Jehovah's chosen spokesman could give. All plans for the invasion of Assyria had been laid. The troops of Israel were in readiness, awaiting only the king's command.

Word from the east continued to confirm Nineveh's desperate condition. The plague that had begun weeks before had nearly paralyzed the capital, laying the imperial hub bare to any invader. If Israel did not strike soon, the Ararat barbarians surely would. Only the distraction of activities along the empire's northern border could have prevented the mountaineers from acting this long.

Jeroboam stepped through the patchy darkness of Jonah's room until he stood within arm's reach of the cloak. It hung limply before him, almost seeming to taunt him with its silence. In awe, he lifted a tremulous hand and stroked it.

"Perhaps he lies dead upon some roadside . . . ," the king whispered. "Is Jonah dead?" he asked aloud.

The mantle made no reply and the monarch pulled away, a dejected tear slipping down one cheek. He turned from the chamber in helpless frustration. He could make no move without the prophet. Yet surely he must. He was destined to lift Israel to glory. Jonah himself had said so.

After passing inland along the African coast, then turning up toward Palestine,

Jonah entered Israel in secret. Although due to the offerings of the superstitious Egyptians, he could have afforded to travel in comfort, he made his way on foot, hidden beneath an updrawn hood.

His appearance had nearly returned to normal by the time he reached his native land. His skin was recovering its healthy olive glow, and he did not veil himself for shame. Rather, he concealed his identity lest Jeroboam discover his homecoming.

Though Jonah was determined to follow the Lord's commission, he would rather die than have the king learn of his destination. How could he ever explain a trek to Nineveh? How could he ever convince the monarch of Israel that Jehovah had commanded he preach to Assyria?

No, it was best that he simply make haste for the east, avoiding detection at all costs.

Still, when he had come upon Samaria this evening, its mount lit tenderly by the seaward moon, he found it impossible to pass by without a pause. He lingered now beyond the shadows of its high walls, upon the western plain — his eyes lifted toward the palace.

He was alone on the highway, and drawing his staff close to his side, he leaned against it, sighing wistfully. He had been certain, as he came near the city, that he had seen a light in the second story window belonging to his own chamber. Surely no maid or manservant would be cleaning the room at this hour. He suddenly realized that Jeroboam himself must have entered the quarters. No one else would have reason to be there.

He ached with sorrow, as he imagined the king's heaviness. Such a quandary the calling of God had posed for all those dear to the prophet! Soon he would be passing near Gath-hepher, and there, too, he would find it necessary to avoid the ones he loved. For how could Amittai ever tolerate such a mission? The idea of the Judean Amos ministering to Israel had been difficult enough for the old man to accept. That his own son should go to Nineveh . . . why, the very notion could break his provincial heart!

The road bid Jonah follow without detour. He studied the familiar ramparts and balustrades of the magnificent Samaritan palace and knew he must not enter. He would require the same caution when nearing the humbler abode of his native village.

As he turned to proceed north, he realized that the comforts of Israel were not to accompany him on this journey. Not even the cloak of Amos would shelter him. He had left it hanging on a hook in the sacred halls of his people's king. And his heart was hung beside it.

CHAPTER
4

It was impossible to travel through Israel
and not hear rumblings of war. It was
spoken in the marketplace of every city, and
whispered upon the housetops of every village. Though there were no weapons
wielded, and though no soldier yet marched
to battle, every Israelite tingled with the anticipation of conflict — and every Israelite's
wife prayed that her man would be spared
the call of duty.

Jeroboam had not yet announced the day
of attack. But it was common knowledge
that his sights were set on Assyria. By the
time Jonah reached the boundary of Lake
Chinnereth and was veering east for
Damascus, he had been apprised of the
king's intentions by fellow travelers at each
oasis, by gatekeepers at each crossroads,
and by gossiping innkeepers from Ibleam
to Hamath. He nearly felt the troops of
Israel breathing on his heels as he trekked

toward the desert.

And he felt once again the lot of the fugitive — as though he bore the mark of crime for his mission. He dare not tell anyone just why his face was turned toward Nineveh. He might as well betray his nation's most covert military secrets, as bear the news of redeeming truth to Assyria.

It was at a resting place somewhere northeast of Damascus that the full irony of God's apparent humor hit him. For failing to see the obvious, he intended never to forgive himself!

It came to him in a flash of insight, sparked by the most mundane observation imaginable — an example in the natural world. Just as he had watched the desert hawk spy out the Egyptian landscape, tonight he watched as a great eagle swooped close to the Syrian wilderness. But this time he was able to see its prey — a small gray hare, darting to and fro beneath the moonlit shadows of the enormous wings.

The rabbit's burrow was plainly discernible in the blue light, a hump of rounded earth in the hollow of a cup-shaped vale. The eagle seemed to tease the poor creature with the nearness of its home, as if daring it to make speed for the sandy sanctuary.

Yet, though the little creature could easily have reached cover, escaping the exposed talons of the predator, it appeared not to trust its own habitat. Perhaps because the retreat was so readily accessible, it was suspect. Or because the eagle seemed to proffer it, rather than distract the rabbit from safety, the diminutive victim ran the other way.

Out across the desert, into the unknown, the furry target raced, directly in line with the bird's spearlike charge. Instantly, it was over, the tiny animal's life snatched with its body high into the air.

"Of course!" Jonah cried, his face a portrait of amazed delight. "Why did I not see it before?"

It was a good thing the prophet was alone. Had any other travelers been nearby, they would have scrutinized him as carefully as the camel drivers who had once questioned his sanity.

Sitting upright, he stirred the flames of a small fire over which roasted a savory meal of grouse and onions. And he stared across the desert toward the target of his own mission.

"I am sent to point the way to truth and

safety, *but Assyria shall reject it!*" he said, slapping his thigh until it stung. "Then, when Israel strikes, it will be for the vindication of God!"

Jonah stood up and paced the desert rise, laughing. His heart surged with relief. "Oh, what trouble I could have spared myself if only I had seen this before! I am not sent to save Nineveh, but to make her condemnation sure!"

CHAPTER
5

The palm-lined rise just outside Nineveh's northern wall was covered with spectators — standing or sitting upon the ground — all in a mood of nervous excitement.

When the emperor could not succeed against a real enemy, a barbarian horde, or a ravaging plague, he resorted to the circus. There he could demonstrate his prowess in the hunt, and establish a measure of credibility as leader of the greatest power on earth.

Ashur-dan was a skilled lion hunter. The fact that his prey were captured for him in the desert mountains, and that they were retained for his spear within wooden cages, did not detract from the spectacle of his arena shows.

The people of his capital were a prime audience for such display. Demoralized by the onslaught of insurmountable forces, they filled the outdoor coliseum, eager for any distraction — however temporary — from their troubles.

On the plain, soldiers with tall body shields ringed a flat, tamped circle of earth, their long spears, held in tight fists, forming a fence about the field.

Already large patches of the park were soaked in blood, and three lion carcasses had been dragged from the arena, cut down by the emperor's aim.

They were local animals, having been captured not far away in the foothills. The day's prize still paced a narrow stall, confined to a crate throughout the show. He was angry and hungry, and when he roared now and then, the crowd roared with him, their lust for his destruction piqued by his torment.

He was a bearded cat, with a magnificent mane and golden coat. But more than this, he was from the vicinity of the barbarian homeland, the distant northern range of Ararat. He symbolized, to the Ninevites, their feared enemies, and they could not wait for Ashur-dan to go against him.

A paltry satisfaction it would be, to see him destroyed. Everyone knew that today's entire affair was mere play-making. But fantasy, when people have no hope, is better than reality.

Ashur-dan had not told the citizens

about his court pronouncement. He had not told them that they would be called upon in just three days to sacrifice their firstborn to the god of Israel.

The six weeks that he had allowed for the plague to lift had nearly passed. And this afternoon's spectacle was the emperor's gift of last rites.

All present had heard of Israel's challenge. Many wondered why no Palestinian lion represented that foe. But the wisemen of Ashur-dan's court knew the reason. He was afraid of the Hebrew god, and dared not offend him.

A small throne had been brought from the palace to the arena, and it sat vacant near the wall of shields, just up the rise. It was Kisha's chair, stationed there as a reminder to all that she lay sick and needed their prayers. When at last no beast but the Ararat cat remained to challenge the monarch, Ashur-dan motioned to the little pedestal.

"For Kisha!" he cried as the magnificent lion shot forth from its opened cage.

The crowd went wild, its voice echoing the king's over and over. "For Kisha! For Kisha!" they chanted, remembering their princess with a fondness reflecting the emperor's heart.

Ashur-dan's stallion stamped and

snorted as the cat rushed across the field. But it did not move as the king's bowman circled and, from the height of his own steed, let fly an arrow to the lion's soft flank. Then, neck arched, the stallion lifted both forefeet, allowing the beast to snap at its hooves — and on the instant Ashur-dan poised his spear.

Another cheer went up from the crowd. The emperor would not play with this quarry. Like a lightning shaft his bronze weapon found its mark, piercing the lion's side, slick and deep. A shooting stream of blood brought the entire audience to its feet; and the royal hounds, released from their leashes, streaked across the park, ripping into the flailing cat and making a quick end to its misery.

The show had served its purpose. The people had forgotten their own sorrows for a few hours. And Ashur-dan was assured an ongoing position in their shallow hearts.

No real glory had been won, however. As the emperor left the arena, to the cheers of thousands, he cast a wary glance west.

Not even in sport could Israel be vanquished. Nor had the hand of the Hebrews' nameless god been lifted from Assyria's capital.

CHAPTER
6

The vast stretch of wilderness between Haran and Nineveh was virtually uninterrupted. The city-state of Gozan lay near Jonah's route, but he skirted it, and was alone with his thoughts for days before reaching the capital.

When he did at last catch his first glimpse of the sprawling city and its neighboring suburbs, he stopped still, breathless with fear and wonder.

Like a string of giant blocks erected by some god-child, the numerous towns of Nineveh stretched across the mountain-rimmed horizon. Never in his wildest imaginings had Jonah conceived the enormity of the enemy's home. With one glimpse he understood why the Assyrian emperors were titled King of the Universe, Master of the World.

Multistoried fortresses ringed the gates of each town, and gleaming edifices, dedicated to commerce and religion, dozed behind them in material contentment. Surveying Nineveh and its environs from this distance, it was hard to believe any trouble existed there — that any political fear could stalk its streets or that plague could thrive within its pristine walls.

"God," the prophet implored, "what can one lone Hebrew say to such a city?"

But he remembered well the Lord's promise when he had renewed the call: ". . . preach unto it the words that I give you!"

And he knew the cry of Nineveh was great, that the true King of the Universe was angry against the Bloody Dog. As he dwelt on these things, he took courage. Though he did not wear the cloak of Amos, he stood tall upon the wilderness road, and threw his shoulders back.

"Forty days," the message came from his own lips. "Forty days and Nineveh shall be overthrown!"

The thought was not his own. He had had enough experience with prophecy to know the source of the declaration. Instantly his mind was filled with a vision: marching troops and dust-raising war machines spread as far as the eye could see, heading from the west along the King's Highway.

"Jeroboam!" he cried. "You shall come against Nineveh at the timing of God!"

With this, he knew what he would say to the citizens of Ashur-dan. If he had before doubted his ability to strike fear in their breasts, his doubts now dissipated. His stark blue eyes focused clearly on his object, and he lifted his staff in a solid grip. With a firm tread, he struck out across the last miles of his mission, ready to declare Assyria's demise.

Within the borders of the white-walled city, there was anything but contentment. Just last evening the emperor's edict had been made public, and sounds of horror filled the streets. Discordant wailing and screams of fear issued from every doorway.

What greeted Jonah, therefore, was more than a plague-ridden metropolis. He had been ready to encounter disease and death. He had girded himself to confront immorality and violence. But he was not prepared to find an audience primed for repentance.

He could not, at first, decipher the cause of the maudlin scene upon which he entered. If sickness were the sole source of these people's misery, they should, after all this time beneath its heavy hand, have settled into a pall of depressed silence, and not be in such an agitated frenzy.

Jonah had begun his trek through Nineveh in the most northerly suburb of Tepe Gawra. Coming upon an arthritic elder at the council benches, he asked him the reason for the terrible noise arising from the streets. The Hebrew was not highly practiced in the Assyrian language, and the old man, noting his broken dialect, immediately placed him as a foreigner.

"You're a fool to enter here," he warned, shaking his head emphatically. "Have you not heard of the disease that takes our youngest and our strongest?"

"Indeed." Jonah nodded. "Who has not? But do you mean to tell me that such a chorus of mourning has persisted here since the plague descended?"

"Oh," the elder whispered, "we are nearly accustomed to the devastation of the air. It is the cruel pronouncement of our king that now tears at our hearts."

"Ashur-dan?" the prophet spurred him. "What pronouncement has he made?"

"Why," the counselor muttered, "our young ruler apparently feels that more death may save this city. He has called for a sacrifice . . . tomorrow at noonday."

"Sacrifice? Of what sort? Surely no

common sacrifice could stir your women to such agony, or your grandfathers to such sadness."

"The firstborn . . . ," the elder explained. A twinge of speechless anger marked his creased face as he considered the emperor's foolishness. But Jonah must hear more.

"Your children?" he groaned. "Ashurdan would surrender your sons and daughters to your gods?" Horror etched his countenance, and the urge to bring vengeance upon this place was nearly overwhelming. Therefore, when the old advisor corrected him, he was stunned.

"Not *our* gods!" the Ninevite said. "Our gods have more sense than to call for the elimination of life in their already languishing capital. No, young man. I can see that you are indeed ignorant of the terror that stalks our streets, and that drives our monarch to this insanity. For it has long since been determined that no deity of the Assyrians has leveled the destroying hand against us. It is the god of an alien tribe who hounds us to the ground. And it is to this deaf and unfeeling star that we will, tomorrow, give up our dearest and our best. If he will not hear us after that, we will lie down quietly to die . . . all of us."

For the first time since Jonah had escaped the whale's belly — for the first time since he had set his feet to fulfill the Lord's commission — he was touched by compassion for the enemy. He had experienced the odd sensation when Ashur-dan had bowed before him in nighttime visitations, when the persistent nightmares had given him fits of insomnia. He had been ashamed of the emotion then. And even now, as the orthodox Hebrew stood on pagan soil, he fought the urge to reach out kindly to this elder Ninevite, to run up and down the streets embracing the brokenhearted and speaking hope to the tormented.

"Tell me, sir," he said with respect, "what strange god provokes the emperor to this madness? Ashur-dan must be dissuaded from this folly."

The Assyrian was incredulous. "How little you know of us or our ways!" he spat. "No one has power to turn the heart of Ashur-dan!"

Jonah bowed reverently and shook his head. "I meant no offense, sir," he assured him. "But I am here on a mission, and I must learn what I can before I seek to perform it."

The counselor drew back, suspicious.

But at last he sighed and shrugged his shoulders. "I do not know what possible difference it can make to you, a stranger to our land. But surely you have heard that the Israelites threaten us from the west?"

"I have."

"Then it should be clear why Ashur-dan suspects their god of this cruelty, and why he wishes to appease him. Though neither I nor his other ministers approve his decision, he feels it best to offer up our first-born on the bloody altar of the Hebrews' faceless Star."

Jonah fell back, a pain shooting through his breast. His face was white as he turned from the elder without another word, and stumbled down the suburb viaduct.

The old fellow scrutinized his odd behavior, and called after him. "Who did you say sent you to Nineveh? And from whence do you hail?" he demanded.

But Jonah did not answer. It would be several hours before he found his voice to say anything, or to cry out against the fallen enemy who groveled all about.

CHAPTER
7

Jonah's heart was a conundrum as he trekked through the suburbs of Nineveh. He could neither entirely love nor completely hate the pathetic inhabitants who watched his passage with hollow and fearful eyes.

He had gone nearly a full day's journey into the metropolis, which sprawled along the Tigris. It was not until he reached the town of Dur Sharrukin, the last before Nineveh itself, that he found strength for the task of preaching.

Two things God had told him to declare: When he first had called Jonah to the mission, he had commanded him to cry against the wickedness of Nineveh. Second, he had informed the prophet that in forty days the place would be overthrown.

A part of Jonah longed to proclaim both, to castigate the oppressors of the nations, to hold before them the enormity of their sin and the impending doom. Another part, however, the part that evoked his sympathies, wished to spare them, to avoid reference to the evil that had brought about their writhing sorrow.

Time was of the essence, however. If, indeed, Ashur-dan had commanded the death of all firstborn for the sake of appeasing Jehovah, the prophet must set matters straight. The God of the Hebrews loathed human sacrifice. In fact, he loved mercy and contrition far more than the blood of goats and rams, and would have disallowed the shedding of any kind of blood — had there been remission of sins through another means. The taking of human life for such a purpose was totally anathema to the Hebrews' God.

Jonah's entire experience, since the day he left Gath-hepher in search of Amos, had been one of ironies and opposites. He had been called to evict a Phoenician queen from Israel's throne, and had then thrust himself on the mercy of Phoenician seamen. He had run from a mission to Gentiles, and his very running had been the vehicle of ministry and conversion to pagan sailors. He had been swallowed by a man-eating whale, only to be spared certain death in the Mediterranean — by the fish itself. And though he had called Jeroboam to raise Israel to her greatest glory, he himself had been called to preach to the targeted enemy.

Now, having surrendered to the will of God, he found his desire to bring down retribution on Assyria being replaced by the paralysis of pity.

He could not sort it all out. Only with the passage of time would he make sense of it. For now, he must act on blind obedience.

He had come to the central square of Dur Sharrukin, and he stood there alone, unheeded by his would-be audience, who faced the coming hours in helpless dread. Taking a deep breath, he opened his mouth. "Forty days!" he cried. "Forty days and Nineveh shall be overthrown!"

He found it necessary to repeat this warning several times before his voice, nearly lost in the din of mourning, captured the ears of those round about.

"Nineveh the Bloody and the Cruel has fallen!" he shouted. "Repent and turn from your wickedness that you may be saved!"

The reaction was predictable. First a stunned silence, then laughter — not so much against the message as the messenger. Who was this strange pilgrim who spoke with a broken accent and dared issue such a warning in a land not his own?

A madman, they deduced — not an uncommon sight in a city touched by raging fever.

But when he identified himself as a "son of Israel, a herald of Jehovah," the mood of the listeners changed.

The God of Israel was the very one to whom they were to give up their children! What fool would dare speak further evil tidings in his name?

Despite Ashur-dan's command to appease this alien deity, Jonah was risking his life representing him. Still he rode the momentum of courage that his obedience sparked. "Your oppressions and your sins stink in the nostrils of God!" he cried. "Turn from your iniquities and be spared!"

There were those who would have pursued him down the avenue. Others would have silenced him with violent hands. But the truth was a shield about him, and he passed toward the capital unscathed.

"Forty days!" he called again. "Forty days and Nineveh shall be overthrown! Turn from your wickedness while there is yet time!"

Women spat upon him from the rooftops and men cursed him as he walked. But no one touched him. And his words echoed unhindered in their ears, long after he had gone his way.

CHAPTER
8

Kisha, in a rare moment of revived strength, sat upon a divan at the arched window of her chamber. Below, in Nineveh's square, a morose but docile crowd had gathered: heartbroken mothers carrying weeping children, or leading their little ones, against their protestations, toward the altar erected at the center.

In many cases, the mothers themselves were led by the men of the families, as they pulled and shoved, trying to shield their babies and elder children from their fate. But the sounds of mourning were tempered by a form of acceptance.

There were others, lingering behind locked doors throughout the city, who would have to be summoned by armed guards. But they were the exception — and by noon, every firstborn male and female, old or young, would be presented for sacrifice.

Only Ashur-dan himself would escape the edict. Though he was the elder child of the royal family, he was the emperor, and his life was sacrosanct.

Kisha thought on her brother with a sigh, the prince who had longed for immortality. Though he would live, she pitied him, for he would carry the memory of this day to his grave.

The sundial in the court of the emperor's ancestors read nearly midday. The princess could see it plainly from this height, where it stood exposed to heaven's brightest lights, both morning and evening.

And she could discern Ashur-dan's steps as he passed her room on his way to the square below.

He halted outside her door, as if he considered seeing her before the appointed horror. But he apparently thought better of it, and continued on his way.

Kisha was relieved to hear his tread die out down the corridor. She could not have helped him, in her weakened condition. And she could not have smiled on his edict. To her mind, no god deserved the lives of innocent children. And if the Star of the Hebrews required it, all Nineveh should die cursing him.

As the sun reached its zenith, the frail girl grew faint. She had asked much of herself to sit up this long. But she could not take her eyes from the pitiful ones beneath her balcony. Her young heart beat fiercely against the cruelty of it all, and she would have blasphemed the Hebrew god aloud, had she only known his name.

Drums in the Nineveh square began to measure the remaining moments. With their deliberate unyielding cadence, the sounds of sorrow grew louder in the streets. Grown men wept, and little girls hid their faces in their mothers' skirts.

The high priest of Asshur, awkward with representing the Unknown God, stepped behind the elevated altar; and as he did so a dizzying pall fell over the crowd. He said nothing, but only lifted his hands, indicating that the moment had arrived. Whimpers broke the silence, and then came screams of terror.

Ashur-dan stood higher than the altar, observing his people's torment with an aching and helpless heart. Then the first child was called forth.

As the pink-cheeked lad ascended the altar steps, his mother clung to him, her husband dragging her away despite her convulsant pleas. And as the boy was bound to the altar, tears poured down the emperor's face.

"Come and save us!" he found himself saying.

Kisha could not hear her brother's prayer, but she sensed his misery as she studied him with tormented eyes. In fact, no one heard him above the din of the perplexed and horrified crowd — no one save the prophet of Jehovah, only now arrived at the palace gate.

Jonah knew that Ashur-dan begged for mercy. He had heard him do so in his dreams, long before the emperor himself had fallen so low. And as he located the monarch, high upon his pedestal, the Hebrew's soul was spurred afresh with compassion.

Indeed, this was the fellow whom he had watched from the Damascus wall. This was the pathetic one who had pleaded with him time and again in the night.

Suddenly Jonah was compelled to intervene.

"Do not touch a hair of the child's head!" the prophet bellowed, his voice overriding all other cries in the city.

The high priest of Asshur stopped the knife in its arc above the rigid body of the intended sacrifice. His stormy gaze sought out the intruder, and when it fell upon Jonah, the old wiseman turned to Ashur-dan in consternation.

"I say, do not touch a hair of the child's head!" Jonah repeated. "Neither lay hold on any son or daughter of your people! For this is not seemly in Jehovah's eyes!"

As the emperor beheld the Hebrew against the far wall of the compound, he was filled with awe. On the instant, he knew him — the one whose memory had haunted him since the night he fled Damascus.

Taking a shaky step forward, the king descended his platform and motioned for the stranger to approach.

The high priest watched this turn of events with speechless wonder, and not without jealousy. Though he had resented the need to represent an alien god, he far more resented the interruption that now took the focus off himself. And he doubted more than ever the emperor's sanity.

But Ashur-dan cared not for public or private opinion. Jonah's words had filled him with hope, and he drew him up by the hands to stand beside him.

The prophet joined him gladly, above the watchful crowd. And as he studied the one who had roused him from sleep so many nights, he could not help but smile.

Nonetheless, the Hebrew's blue eyes pierced the emperor's soul, and suddenly Ashur-dan was on his knees, kissing the floor before Jonah and caressing the holy man's feet with his tears. "A long time have we waited, my lord," the monarch wept. "Only speak, and we shall do whatever you command!"

Jonah could not think deeply on the task Jehovah had given him. Had he done so, he would only have run from it again. But running had caused him too much grief in the past.

The words came easily to him, for they were not his words.

"Turn from iniquity, and from the worship of false idols," he demanded. "The One True God, Jehovah, stands ready to redeem and to heal. And he seeks not your sacrifices; but a broken and a contrite heart are his reward."

CHAPTER
9

That evening a fast was declared throughout Nineveh.

After Jonah had confronted the king upon his platform, calling a halt to the sacrifices and imploring the monarch to obey the True God, the prophet had been escorted into the palace. There, just as in Israel, he was afforded a comfortable chamber and was treated royally.

Ashur-dan had retired to his own quarters, and after a long while he entered the throne room, calling for the Hebrew.

The central hall of Samaria's palace could not begin to rival the magnificence of this arched and pillared gathering place. Behind the emperor's great chair was a sweep of glazed tile, lapis lazuli blue, covering an entire wall. Upon it were, arrayed in fine detail, artistic representations of kingly deeds and heroic legends. A deep carpet of the same blue, figured in reds and golds, led from the throne to the floor of the chamber, and robed the whole stage upon which the king sat.

Ashur-dan himself was garbed in the finest wine velvet, silver tassels decorating each seam and fold. Upon his head sat the ancestral crown, tall and shining, inset with precious gems.

Jonah was dazzled by the finery, and he stood silent before his host. But more awe-provoking than all the gold of Assyria and its crafted wonders were the monarch's words. Motioning the Hebrew to step close, he leaned down from his throne. "I have spent these past hours since noon in private prayer to the Unknown God . . . to this 'Jehovah' of the Hebrews," he said.

The name of the Lord sounded strange when spoken by the Assyrian. The emperor spoke it awkwardly, but it bore a musical quality when imbued with his native accent. Jonah bowed his head graciously and nodded.

"I am poorly educated in his ways, as you must surely know," the ruler admitted. "Yet I realize that the path my people have followed is contrary to his holiness."

Jonah could not refute him, and so only nodded again. Then, squaring his shoulders, he asserted, "To you, O Highness,

Jehovah has been unknown. But he is not unknowable. Set all your other gods aside, and you shall find him. For he is the One and Only True God."

Ashur-dan chafed at the declaration. But he could not argue with it. What, after all, had any of his many deities done for Nineveh when they were needed most? And who could deny that this lone stranger bore the truth in his very bones? Jonah was a man of few words, but the words he spoke were God-given, and he himself had been sent to a field ripe for conquest.

"We are ready to do as you bid," the emperor insisted. "Only speak the command, and we shall obey."

Jonah studied the pained fervor with which the monarch made this assertion. The urgency recalled to him the several dreams in which his heart had been moved toward this Gentile. But before the prophet could speak, the king took it upon himself to prove his own sincerity.

Throughouts this brief interview, several members of the royal cabinet had been standing near. Apparently primed for their master's direction, they moved quickly when he clapped his hands, and scurried to bring a small cart from a side room.

Jonah watched in amazement as the little

table was uncovered, revealing a large urn full of ashes with a pile of sackcloth beside it. Ashur-dan clapped his hands again, and the ministers hurried to his stage, where he now had stood up from his throne. With determined fingers, the emperor was unclasping the great buckle which secured his heavy velvet robe about his shoulders. He let it fall to the floor, where his companions quickly retrieved it for safe-keeping.

Next the ministers carried to him the large swaths of burlap; and after he had donned them, he walked toward the balcony that commanded a view of the public courtyard.

Hundreds of his citizens still waited there, having kept vigil until their monarch should return with word of his intentions. When he appeared, touched by the sunset light and garbed in the humblest of raiment, their hearts were strangely stirred. A hushed awe overcame them, and then a mighty cheer arose from the people, as from one body.

Once more Ashur-dan clapped his hands. The congregation grew silent as the urn was brought forth and its contents sprinkled upon the balcony floor. Through the grate of the porch the people watched as their master seated himself upon the ash heap.

"I have spent my life longing for glory," the monarch shouted, his voice carrying like the cry of a desert bird over the house-tops. "But let it be said of Ashur-dan that his greatest achievement was repentance! For I see now that all our misbegotten ways and the ways of our forefathers offend the Lord of the Universe!"

The audience did not take their eyes from him as he lifted a handful of dust from the floor and sifted it through his hair, heavy tears coursing down his cheeks.

"In Nineveh," he declared, "by the decree of the king and his nobles: Do not let man, beast, herd, or flock taste a thing. Do not let them eat or drink water. But both man and beast must be covered with sackcloth. And let men earnestly call on the Only True God, Lord Jehovah of the Hebrews, that each may turn from his wicked way and from violence. For it may be," he concluded, "God will turn and relent, and withdraw his burning anger so that we shall not perish!"

While a scribe took down every word so that copies of the edict might be sent throughout the capital, another ear-shattering cheer rose from the congregation.

If fasting and sackcloth would please their king, and if this strange god, Jehovah, were now his god, the people would repent in kind. Of the Unknown Deity they were ignorant; but he had returned to them their firstborn, and had rebuked the bloody sacrifice. Therefore they were ready to follow him, and to learn all his ways.

CHAPTER
10

Jonah stood at the rail of his private balcony, his gaze westward and his fists clenched. Though he had every reason to be happy, his choice to follow the Lord's commission having met with incredible success, he was overwhelmed by a nameless depression.

There were no fellow prophets in whom he could confide, or who might explain to him the shameful anger that possessed him. To his knowledge, no seer save Amos had ever been sent outside his own nation. "And at least Amos preached to fellow Hebrews," he muttered.

The bitterness in that thought should have been revealing, but Jonah did not hear himself.

Had his way not been smooth here? Had his message not fallen on ready ears, and met with a reception any other preacher would have envied? What was wrong with him, that he could not revel in the healing and conversion of 120,000 pagan souls?

Very little had been required of him since arriving in the imperial capital. A few words spoken in the streets, and at the ripe time upon an Assyrian stage, a brief meeting with the emperor — and all had been accomplished.

Perhaps the very ease of it all was part of the problem. After so much struggle, after his cowardly fight and the tortures at sea, after weeks of battling against the call of God, his entire purpose had been accomplished in one breath.

Yes, this was that depression that follows on the heels of tremendous stress, whether it be from a positive or a negative experience.

But there was more to his condition than letdown.

Jonah was jealous. As the weeks had worn on since the first day of the fast, he had sensed the sprouting and then the tangled growth of irrational envy deep within his heart. The more news had been brought to him of spiritual revival in this alien land, and the more he had been confirmed as a minister to Gentiles, the more he had resented his lot. Repeatedly his thoughts turned homeward, and the old longing to see Jeroboam trample the Easten Dog obsessed him.

How could he admit such disparity? Yet he was torn by it. For he did love Ashurdan. He had great compassion for the Ninevites who had wandered so many centuries in darkness. But he was first an Israelite, and then a herald of Jehovah.

"My God," he whispered, suddenly faced squarely with his own idolatry. "Can it be . . . ?"

Introspection was cut short by a knock on his chamber door. And presently, the lilting voice of Princess Kisha pressed through the portal. "Yuna," she called, filling his name with Assyrian music.

The prophet's heart surged. The young girl had a way with him that he had experienced with no other female. And he *had* spent a good deal of time with her since dwelling here.

The moment she had seen him in the Ninevite square, she testified, the sickness had lifted from her body. And as the plague had been eradicated throughout the city, she had regained her strength as though she had never been touched by the scourge.

She was now very devoted to the prophet, her "messenger dove," as she interpreted his name. As devoted to "Yuna" as he was to Israel. And she represented to him his dilemma more perfectly than even her brother could do.

Jonah hesitated to answer her summons. Perhaps he should pretend to be asleep, or away from his room entirely. But the thought of her soft, dark eyes convinced him otherwise.

"Enter, my lady," he replied, turning from the balcony with a sigh.

Eagerly, she opened the door. As always, her handmaid accompanied her, for propriety's sake. But in spirit she was alone with the man, and she swept across the room on winged feet, embracing him joyfully.

Jonah tried to hold her at arm's length. But she resisted his attempt, and pressed into his bosom like a small child.

"Oh, Yuna!" she lisped. "You old hermit! You have been cloistered away all day! Dan and I are missing you."

Then pulling him to a divan, she gazed excitedly into his troubled eyes. "Why did you never tell me?" she rebuked him.

"Tell you what?"

"Of your adventure with Leviathan!" Her face was radiant with enthusiasm for the subject, and she shook her head with a scowl. "You would share such a tale with Dan and keep it from me? I am very angry, Yuna!"

Jonah laughed, taking her small hands in his. "Your brother is most inquisitive, my lady. He asks a good many questions, and I give him the necessary answers."

Then, rising from the sofa, the prophet tried not to be overly taken by her attentions. "Besides," he insisted, "I came to your land only to speak my message, and not to point to myself."

Kisha was wounded by the rebuff, and looked sadly at the floor. For a long moment silence passed between them, until Jonah glanced her way again. "Oh, dear child," he sighed, "think nothing of my moods. I do not even understand them myself, most times."

He sat beside her once more, and she raised her face to his, leaning a bit closer than he wished. The small-girl excitement returned. "A whale? You dwelt inside a whale's belly for three days?"

"I did," he acknowledged, ashamed to tell her that his escapade was the result of disobedience. "Had I known that such folk as yourself waited for me here, I never would have delayed and gone through such hell. . . ."

His voice was so low, she almost missed his confession. But she sensed his shame, and, though not understanding it, did not press him further.

"Then," she whispered, her eyes wide with awe, "you are more than a prophet. You are more even than a messenger dove!"

Jonah hesitated to hear more. Her adulations were an embarrassment, and he sensed a greater one coming.

"*You are one raised from the dead!* Three days dead, and raised again, to give my people life eternal!"

The prophet could bear no more. A hollow groan escaped him.

"You think too highly of me, my lady," he cried. "Go now . . . and let me be."

The young woman studied him miserably. But as she stood to leave, she watched his sad return to the balcony, the very mystery of the man binding her heart more fondly to him.

CHAPTER
11

Jonah's heartsickness did not lift. His longing continually turned to Israel, toward the king whom he had groomed for glory.

The fact that Jeroboam still did not know his whereabouts, and dread that he would inevitably learn of the prophet's outreach in Nineveh, troubled him beyond expression. He felt that he could not again, after ministering to the hated Assyrians, set foot in his own homeland. Surely, at least, he would never again be welcome in the halls of Samaria.

It was the deep of night over the capital. Kisha had left him hours ago, and he had not moved from his room all day or all evening.

With trembling hands, he packed a bag with scraps left over from his dinner, and he wadded a supply of clothing around the morsels. He intended to secrete himself in the desert, to sit out the coming weeks until the forty prophesied days should pass. If, as he feared, God had withdrawn his hand of retribution from the repentant empire, and if Jeroboam had not marched upon Nineveh by that time, he would just as soon die as ever go home.

If only his words had fallen on stony hearts! If only the ears of the Ninevites had been closed to the truth! Then it would not matter that he had betrayed the trust of Israel. He could excuse his mission as the ultimate condemnation of his nation's pagan oppressors.

But the monarch of Assyria had repented! Who would have ever thought . . . ?

Jonah cursed the stubborn satchel as it strained at the seams against his stock of supplies. "Please, Lord, was not this what I said while I was still in my own country?" he ranted. "In order to forestall this very thing, I fled to Tarshish! For I knew that you are a gracious and compassionate God, slow to anger and abundant in loving-kindness — and one who relents concerning calamity!"

The embittered prophet slung the heavy bag over his shoulder and snuffed out the light at his bedside. "Now, O Lord, please take my life from me!" he cried. "For death is better to me than life!"

Stumbling toward the door, he unbarred it and stood shaking in the shadows.

Suddenly a warm breeze parted his curtains, riding the light of the desert moon to his very shoulder. "Do you have good reason to be angry?" it whispered.

Jonah had heard that voice before. He recognized it as belonging to Jehovah, and his heart stopped.

But he could bear not another syllable, and stepping through the portal, he made haste for the eastern horizon.

He had trekked far into the desert by dawn. As the morning sun reached its zenith, he ceased his thoughtless wandering.

His skin had been unusually sensitive to long exposure ever since his acidic adventure in the whale's belly. Quickly he scrambled to create himself a shelter.

Only round tumbleweeds suggested building material, and he hurriedly gathered several together, tangling them against one another, until a low wall and then a hint of a roof faced back toward the sprawling capital. Taking from his satchel one of the thick garments which Ashur-dan had given him, he threw it over the pathetic lean-to and slipped beneath its shadow.

His situation was a familiar one by now: fugitive and vagabond, a man without a country. Heavy tears poured down his face as he remembered the little booths he and Amittai had always constructed during the Festival of Tabernacles, when all Hebrew fathers and sons recalled together the wilderness wanderings of Moses and his people. He doubted now that he would ever again commemorate anything religious with his own kind.

Billows of self-pity overswept him. He would have preferred to be dead at sea, to have been digested by briny waves, or by the juices of Leviathan's maw.

Amittai could have built him a fine shelter. He remembered the old man's nimble fingers, their artistic ways with goat's hair and tarpaulins. One of the craftsman's tents would have restrained the invading sun far better than this haphazard hut.

For hours he stewed in self-indulgent sorrow, the heat pressing in on his rebellious skin. Streams of searing sunlight taunted him, ripping through the shelter and through his clothing as though he sat naked.

As he grew faint, wishing again simply to die, a rustling filled his ears. "The wings of the Angel of Death," he whispered.

Then darkness overtook him, and coldness like the tomb.

In the relief that only the surrender of life can bring, he lay down to meet the end. But the longer he waited, the more his spirit revived.

Once before he had accepted a premature demise. Once before he had calculated that death and the grave were his lot, only to learn that the tomb was, to his spirit, a womb — and that he was, in fact, alive.

Now, as he regained his strength, he realized that the coolness on his skin was cast from a shady bower, that the darkness that relieved his eyes was but a leafy shadow, and the rustling of angel wings was the sudden growth of a desert pumpkin plant just outside his hovel.

Stretching his cramped legs, he poked his head beyond the low roof and gazed in speechless wonder upon the God-given comforter.

"Deliverer!" he cried, crawling to the plant on hands and knees. "Surely you are a sign from the Lord!"

Throughout the hottest hours of afternoon, he sat in blissful ease beneath the heaven-sent vine. If Jehovah had been so gracious, perhaps he could yet expect the fulfillment of his fondest hopes.

Perhaps if he rested here long enough, he would yet see Jeroboam's troops march on Nineveh. Though the city had repented, the nation had a long record of sins to account for. And nothing in prophecy firmly denied the possibility that calamity would yet descend.

With nightfall, the Hebrew curled into a peaceful slumber, wrapping the gigantic gourd leaves about his shoulders and dreaming of Israel's glory.

By morning the plant had been destroyed. Jonah awoke with a jolt to the horrifying sound of a thousand caterpillars devouring its leaves and stalk.

Leaping to his feet, he brushed the demonic creatures from his arms and legs with panicky vengeance. In moments, the miraculous vegetation had withered, leaving nothing but a stump and a pile of flaky rubble where it had so majestically flourished.

When the sun had fully risen, a scorching east wind howled about him, the heat of day beating down upon the prophet until he crumpled to his knees. Through blurred vision, he surveyed the eerie landscape, nearly fainting once again.

Even had he wished to return to Nineveh, he had no strength to do so. He fell face first upon the shrunken gourd and drew its litter to his breast, weeping and begging with all his soul to die.

"A cruel God you are, to offer hope and then snatch it away!" he groaned. "Surely death is better to me than life!"

The howling wind grew louder, and with it the voice as in his chamber invaded his consciousness.

"Do you have good reason to be angry about the plant?" it demanded.

This time Jonah knew he must answer, that he dare not avoid the inquisition.

But it was not in humility that he would do so. Lifting a fist to the dusty sky, he challenged, "Indeed! I have good reason to be angry, even to death!"

The elements suddenly ceased their warfare, as an ominous silence overtook the wilderness. Jonah's skin stood in goose prickles, and he hid his tearful face in his hands.

"You had compassion on the plant," the voice returned, "for which you did not labor, and which you did not cause to grow, which sprang up overnight and perished overnight. Should I, then, God of

Nations, who raises kings and lowers them — should I not have compassion on Nineveh, the Great City, in which there are more than 120,000 persons who do not know their right hand from their left."

Jonah shrunk from the exposure. Suddenly, too much was clear, and he feared to lift his eyes.

"You rebuke me for giving you hope with the gourd, and then denying it. Yet," Jehovah concluded, "you would have held out the light of truth to the Gentiles, only to condemn and not to save!"

PART FIVE

RESURRECTION

*There is neither Jew
nor [Gentile] . . .
for ye are all one in
Christ Jesus.
For he is our peace,
who hath made both
one, and hath broken
down the middle
wall of partition
between us.*

GALATIANS 3:28;
EPHESIANS 2:14

CHAPTER
1

Weak with shame and exhaustion, the prophet of Israel, messenger to Nineveh, drifted into a restless slumber upon the desert floor. Evening had come, bringing with it the relief of a cooling breeze. But Jonah's mind swung between sad dreams and pleas for forgiveness until the moon woke him.

He had never felt more the part of an alien on the earth. He did not know whether he should return to Nineveh on the morrow, or try to reclaim a place in Israel.

For a long time he peered miserably across the wilderness, surveying the metropolis in which he had ministered. The withered gourd brushed his arm as the breeze moved it, a pathetic reminder of his failure as a chosen vessel. Indeed, he reasoned, he *was* a failure of the worst sort. For though his mission had won the souls of thousands, his own heart had steeled itself against them.

Were he but given a second chance, he would do his calling justice. Yes, he vowed, he would show forth the *love*, as well as the truth of God.

Jonah clasped his knees to his chin and waited. He did not know what he waited for, until he saw a movement along the foot of the distant wall. White and shimmering, something caught starlight as it traveled out across the desert from the city — from beneath the low "needle's eye" beside the eastern gate.

It was a good while in coming, for Jonah was a long way from town. But as it drew near, it took on recognizable form.

How Kisha had thought to look for him here, he could not imagine. She came unaccompanied, bearing beneath her arm a bundle of some sort. And when she spied him, hunched beneath his crude shelter, she began to run.

"Yuna! Yuna!" she cried. "I knew I would find you beyond the wall! I told my brother you are a solitary man!"

Falling to her knees beside him, she kissed his feet and then clutched his dry hands to her face. "Two days we have sought you! Surely you will return?"

Jonah did not know what to say. He was overwhelmed with her concern, and shame filled him afresh. He could only shake his head, until she lifted the unidentified parcel in her arms and held it forth reverently.

"I knew you would want this, though I do not know what it is," she explained. "It comes with the words of your king, all the way from Israel."

"Jeroboam?" the Hebrew cried.

"The same." She smiled as he grabbed for the package and began to fumble with its silken wrapper. "A strange message he delivered to my brother and to you. It seems that God has turned his heart toward peace since he heard of your labors here. He sends not his troops to our city. Instead he sends this gift, direct to 'his prophet.' "

Jonah ripped at the cover with trembling fingers. Tearing it open, he found inside a large piece of cloth, ragged and dusty.

His pulse sped as he unrolled the material, and leaping to his feet, he unfurled the cloak of Amos!

From a fold of the garment, a small piece of parchment fluttered to the desert floor, and he reached for it, his heart in his throat.

"What does it say?" the princess inquired, noting Jonah's tear-filled expression.

The prophet tried not to stammer as he read the message, though his soul was flooded with wonder. "It says, 'In the mantle of truth lies Israel's greatest glory,' " he whispered.

Kisha stood beside him now, her arm about his bent shoulders. She did not ask the interpretation, but only held him close.

"You must stay and be our teacher," she insisted, leading him slowly toward the imperial walls. "We have very much to learn of your god and his ways."

Jonah drew himself upright and smiled. No one had more to learn than he.

Like donning a piece of home, he pulled the priceless cloak over his back. Beneath the light of heaven, the gates of Nineveh were not so alien.

Jesus said:

The men of Nineveh shall rise in judgment
with this generation, and shall condemn it:
because they repented at the preaching
of Jona[h]; and, behold, a greater than
Jona[h] is here.
For as Jona[h] was three days and three
nights in the whale's belly;
so shall the Son of man
be three days and three nights
in the heart of the earth.

MATTHEW 12:41, 40

And being made perfect,
[Jesus] became the author
of eternal salvation
unto all them that obey him.

HEBREWS 5:9